Lock Down Publications and Ca$h Presents

WHITE BOYS

Written By

BANDEMIC

First Edition 2026

Printed in the United States of America

Lock Down Publications
P.O. Box 944
Stockbridge, GA 30281
www.lockdownpublications.com

Like our page on Facebook: Lock Down Publications
www.facebook.com/lockdownpublications.ldp

Stay Connected with Us!

Text **LOCKDOWN** to 22828 to stay up-to-date with new releases, sneak peaks, contests and more…

Like our page on Facebook:
Lock Down Publications

Join Lock Down Publications/The New Era Reading Group

Visit our website:
www.lockdownpublications.com

Follow us on Instagram:
Lock Down Publications

Email Us: We want to hear from you!

Acknowledgements

This novel is dedicated to my favorite aunt, Rita Young-Chapman. Thank you for your unyielding support of my writing.

To my mother and best friend, Nicilee Brooks. It's a blessing to have such a strong, humorous woman for a mother. Thank you for not giving up on me.

My cousin Shaimon Bristol, who is more like a brother. Thanks for the love and support. You 1 hunnid.

My other brothers from another mother, Eric Jones (E-Money), Labaron Freeman (Nutzo), and Dwayne Warfield. Y'all like blood to me. Thanks for forever keeping it a band.

And my Brandy 'Flake' Lance - forever my heart. Thank you for everything. You're a jewel shorty, and I was lucky to had had you so intimately in love with my crazy ass. Lol.

Shoutout to my dawg, James Oxendine (Cold Ox), and his potential candidate/rotating crown movement on YouTube. We've come a long way from trapping and rapping on that damn Karaoke. Lol.

To my dear friend, Tonya Shade (T-Baby), you are an incredible woman who is beautiful on the inside and out. Thank you for so much.

Then there is Tameka L. White, the queen of the buck. The last time I came home you held me down like a paperweight. Thank you. You are a tremendously loving person with the coolest personality ever.

To my niece, Janae Brooks and my nephew, Jaelin Bradley. You two are like a daughter and son to me. Thanks for the love.

My baby girl, Nicole Kurlee. You've had my back and loved me since we were 13 yrs old. Thank you for never letting go and being a friend first. You're special, and the funniest woman ever. Stay beautiful.

Coy Stieglbauer. Thank you for taking the time to comb through my manuscript for grammatical errors. It was a great job.

What up to: Deangelo Brooks, Kita Bristol, Pooh Roller, Sandy Wallen, Anthea Carter, Patricia Carter, Octavia Hayden, Jeff Smith, T. Hicks (Piggy) Mike Ray, Whitley Grindstaff, Antoria 'Lil Bit' Woods, Lurk, J'Nice, Trap, Keisha 'Butta' Williams, Tashina 'T.T' McElroy, Trell Hicks, James Black, Lorenzo & Andrea, Tina Young, Pooh Stewart, Nikita Biber, Jerry Chapman, David Miller (Big Rula), Jorge Gonzales, Rebecca 'Nikki' Smith, Andrea Langendorf, Keva Garnette, Fat Baby, Kenny 'Head' Tabor, Hancy Black, Michelle Blevins, Chris Washington, Marty Hughes, Wanda Bunche, Sally White, AShley Brooks, Wiggy & Zay, Bobby Johnson.

Special thanks to my main man, Jovoski Barnes (The Mover & Shaker of the Eastern Shores) You were a lot of help, bro! Stay 1 hunnid.

Big ups to the following: Terrence Smith (*Souls* restaurant owner and entrepreneur) Stephen Israel (The daring Israelite) Kenneth Cooper (The O.G) La'Junior (The DMV Striver) Anton Brown (Rock) Chris Estes (The man to know) Curtis Terrell (Bushwick) Terrence Pem. Sean Lashley (Black Yota) Daryl Duboise.

Chapter 1

Teddy Lee, a burly man with sleepy eyes and a short temperament, stood there patiently as his boys—Jim Bob and Cunningham—beat the living hell out of Dog Man, who was bound to a tree by rope. It was a shivery morning, indeed, but Dog Man had stared into the eyes of someone who was much colder—Teddy Lee.

With the filter of a Marlboro balanced between his lips, Teddy Lee held form to the handle of his miniature sledgehammer. He was not a man who sniveled over spilled milk. His family unfortunately lost control of the area—violently removed from the ranks by rival biker gangs who had succumbed to their own horrible demise over the years. However, Teddy Lee was here to take it back, and anyone who refuses to step down will die—simple as that. Teddy Lee was an adamant man, but an idealist in the same instance. He didn't see any sense in killing a perfectly good dealer who has no quarrel with being reduced to a minion who serves him and his cause; the likes of them shall be spared.

Teddy Lee turned his back to the brutal assault to take a gander at the hills. High Knob Mountain overlooked several states: Tennessee, Kentucky, and North Carolina—an astonishing viewpoint of nature. The slopes that were burdened with bear tracks. The rocky cliffs that gave footing to the hawks, and the tranquility of watching the clouds roll in doused his rage with fond childhood memories of his heyday in Lee County.

Looking down at his boots, Teddy Lee nudged a few pine cones while thinking about his brothers and how they used to race throughout the forest as kids en route to their grandfather's cotton gin. He missed those two knuckleheads—their murders affected him the most.

Teddy Lee inhaled some smoke, taking a moment to consider the error of his ways. He was a two-time loser who was beyond reform. Even after completing a 17-year sentence in a maximum-security prison, Teddy Lee only worsened. He came from a long line of criminals. By the age of twelve, he was running moonshine to Asheville, North Carolina, with his uncle, Roach, and aunt Cherle, at which time he consumed his first Quaalude and discovered that he liked the effect of drugs—a lot. That's when he eventually embarked onto a darker path.

Teddy Lee's father, a man who had the sentiment of a sidewinder, was the founder and leader of the notorious local biker gang, '*White Infidels*'—a botched-up organization of hopped-up meth addicts with guns. A thorn that was forced upon Teddy Lee as he sat wasting away in a cell, grieving the deaths of his family.

But now he was finally home, and it was time to take back what was his.

When President Obama was in office, he passed a Clean Bill Act that drove a dagger into the heart of Southwest, Virginia. Coal mining was the bread and butter of the area, so once the mines were forced to close their shafts, the local economy crumbled like a stale slice of Mammaw's sugar cake, leaving a gaping wound that was quickly infested by the drug trade.

Families packed up and set sail, abandoning their homes, which were eventually occupied by squatters who normally converted the once-lovely abode into meth labs or crack hubs. But most of the towns in the region slowly recovered and made a means for their natives.

Lee county was not as fortunate, but Teddy Lee was bent on reviving the glory days of his beloved hometown.

Teddy Lee flicked his cigarette, then turned on the heels of his boots.

Dog Man was taking his punishment like a man, but that was of no surprise—he was built Ford Tough, just like his brothers who all boldly refused to turn over their reign of Norton and Big Stone Gap. So all five of them must be led out to the pasture and put down.

Zipping his coat, Teddy Lee lowered his head and hunkered down against the trying winds. The forest was dead and as still as a scarecrow in a barren cornfield. There was not a more ideal location for murder.

"All right," Teddy Lee said, adjusting his Stetson. "Reckon that's enough, boys."

Jim Bob and Cunningham backed off, both harboring a grit with busted knuckles. Dog Man spat to the ground, a cusp of a tooth lying within the thick red glob.

Teddy Lee approached his captive.

Through swollen slits, Dog Man eyed the sledgehammer. He was afraid. Finally, Teddy Lee could smell it on him—gifts of a predator.

Dog Man was a loner and a genius in his own right when it came to cooking methamphetamine, so targeting him first made more sense, because he was the key player in him and his brothers' operation.

"Reckon you still ain't willing to spill that recipe, are ya', boy?" Teddy Lee wanted to know. "Still wanna lie to ol' Teddy."

Dog Man had discovered a chemical compound that enhanced the quality of his ice, heroin, and cocaine without the downside effect of mixing something as lethal as fentanyl or PCP.

Dog Man spit in his face, then snapped, saying, "Do what you will, you cock-bleeding sumbitch. But I promise you, my brother's gone—"

Teddy Lee swung his mighty hammer into Dog Man’s rib cage, and a sickening crack sounded. Dog Man’s mouth popped wide and a guttural gasp escaped his throat.

“Tell Satan I sent you, boy,” Teddy Lee said through clenched teeth. “I know ’em personally.”

Chapter 2

Later That Day

Country music played from a vintage record player in the living room of the trailer, and Blue, that good ol' bloodhound of Cammy's, was lying at the bedroom door waiting to be fed.

On the opposite side of the door, Cammy was positioned on all fours as Rock-on tongue-kissed her honeypot hungrily. Cammy's expression was transfixed in a veil of ecstasy as her double D's slightly swung to and fro—luscious pink nipples brushing against the sheet—arousing her even more.

Cammy's sugar plum was warm, wet, and deliciously rare in color. Rock-on swallowed every drop of her—rod throbbing, veiny, seeping pre-cum, ready for entry.

Streams of pale moonlight poured through the naked windows by buckets, influencing the candlelit ambiance of sexual obedience and just good ol'-fashioned freakiness.

Easing his thumb into her back door, he spit on her cherry, then began targeting her swollen clitoris—sucking and nibbling her honeysuckle while inciting the juices of her rear canal.

"Fuck," Cammy murmured pleasantly, feeling the pressure mount. "Rock," she shouted, clawing the sheet, arching as an intense climax took her breath.

Rock-on turned Cammy over onto her back, crossed her legs Indian style, and pushed them up against her stomach. Her cookie smiled at him, frosted with blonde peach fuzz, pouting for a kiss, but his handle was crying for relief. Driving his banana inside her pudding, they both moaned pleasurably. Rock-on gyrated his hips, hitting her left wall, then her right, before drilling for oil.

"Harder," Cammy demanded, loving the sensation of pain and desire. "Harder."

Rock-on held her legs down while watching the vibrations of his thrust cause her cheeks to ripple. Balls deep, flesh against flesh, emitting a moist echo in their ears.

Then Rock-on's phone rang. He looked over to the nightstand at the luminous screen and saw that it was his wife, Savannah, calling. He let the call go to voicemail, but she called directly back. Rock-on stepped back, exiting Cammy in one swift motion while reaching for his device.

"It's my wife," he told Cammy. "Not a peep."

This upset Cammy, because although she had accepted the role of his mistress, she hadn't completely gotten over the feeling of being number two. Cammy was just as beautiful as Savannah, just as hardworking and loyal as well, but Rock-on refused to place her in the same bracket as his beloved fucking Savannah—and it pissed her off.

"Hey, hon?" Rock-on answered.

"Rock," Savannah said in a choked-up tone of voice.

Rock-on spoke urgently. He heard tears in her voice. "Darling, what's wrong?"

Sniffles.

"Savannah?"

"It's Dog Man."

The mention of his brother caused his heart rate to quicken—this was it. The Feds must've finally gathered enough evidence to indict them.

"He's dead."

Rock-on's mouth fell open. "What?"

Chapter 3

The *Ride 'em Cowboy, Billiard & Bar* was an eye-capturing 8,000 sq. ft. boomerang-shaped building that was perched on a grassy knoll of cattle—painted in Sudbury yellow with overhanging balconies and Olympian torches for exterior warmth throughout wintry months. In the distance lay the town of Norton, glowing like a flightless firefly on a lily pad.

Davie pulled into the parking lot in his red, tricked-out F-150 on 44" Super Swamp tires. The dual pipes growled harmoniously as the luminary sidebars flickered a vivid neon blue. A country song blared from the Pioneer woofers, and two women stood up from a bench to dance provocatively to the melodic tune that everyone had come to love. Their names were Mindy and Jenna—pill whores who commonly resided at the Duffield jail. Troublesome two.

Davie grinned lustfully, because vivacious floozies were always on the menu. Jenna and Mindy were both wearing extremely tight blue jeans with loose-fitting blouses that awarded a grand view of their cleavage. They were obviously drunk and in search of recreational drugs and sex.

Davie hopped down from the cab of his truck and was overtaken by a coarse gust of wind that entailed the stench of manure. Davie, although gracefully tall and muscular, was considered a *Himbo*—attractive but unintelligent—and if it weren't for his brothers who kept their family afloat through ill-gotten gains, Davie would've been nothing short of a moocher, dependent upon some carefree woman with a good heart.

Davie brushed the sleeves of his neatly tucked flannel shirt, then looked down at his snakeskin boots admiringly. He was a snazzy dresser who held no expense to clothing or anything else, for that matter.

Placing his Stetson on his head, he looked at Jenna and Mindy with a perfect white smile.

"Howdy, girls," he said, tipping the brim of his hat.

"Hey, Davie," they said simultaneously with huge smiles on their faces.

"What you doing tonight, sugar?" Jenna asked him, lowering her eyes to his private section. "Or should I ask, who are you doing tonight?"

Davie licked his lips seductively. Jenna was simply mouthwatering, but he normally had to remind himself of the years when Jenna and his brother, Rock-on, were swapping spit—at which time he would immediately dismiss the urge to rip her clothes from her magnificent body and devour her wildflower. He didn't trail behind kinfolk—ever. His pa' used to always say, *"A nonjudgemental dick has the worst judgement of them all, Davie,"* and he lived by his father's wisdom.

However, Mindy was exceptionally sexy as well, and although she had numerous relationships with both men and women around Norton, none were apples from his family tree, so she was fair game if all else failed tonight.

Reaching inside his pants pocket, Davie said with a flirtatious smirk, "The night's young, sweetheart." He tossed Jenna a small baggie. "So don't run off too far, hear?" He winked at Mindy. "I might have a few ideas."

Jenna looked at the shard of ice, then to Mindy, who could hardly contain her excitement. Davie and his brothers sold the best quality drugs in the region, but their product wasn't cheap—and Davie was the only one who willingly gave people a break, which was why he was everyone's favorite of the siblings.

"We'll be right here," Jenna said, suddenly eager to get to her car where her glass pipe waited.

Entering the bar, Davie took a look around. Ol' Harold Wilson was riding the mechanical bull, and like always, he was aiming to beat Dog Man's top score—never. Pool balls cracked. Laughter, shouting, music, and a whole lot of dancing.

Janice Miller spotted Davie from the upper level and blew him a kiss. Janice was his Kryptonite—that one true gal for him—but Davie had a personal issue with the grounds of commitment that hindered the growth of any monogamist relationship he had ever encountered.

At the tender age of ten years old, Davie was on his way to his Aunt Carol's house to lay with his cousins, Bryce and Shelton, when he decided to take a detour through a wooded grove—a decision that, to this very day, affects him. In those particular woods, Davie saw his sweet, wholesome mother having sex with his father's best friend, who lived on the next street over and was actually married himself. Davie recalled backtracking out of the grove so as not to be seen, but the visual of his mother in that unlikely position had never escaped him. And although Davie had not spoken of that day to anyone, it's the sole reason he doesn't trust women as far as he can throw them.

Smiling to Janice, Davie made his way to the nearest bar. Cigarette smoke layered the atmosphere in a disk, more evident toward the lighting that fled the billiard area slightly shy of the kitchen door.

"Davie," said a man who was seated at the bar.

"Tiny," Davie responded.

"Bigman," said another.

Davie nodded respectfully and said, "How's it going, Joe?"

Davie stopped to speak quietly to a woman who slipped a hundred-dollar bill into his pocket in exchange for drudge. Davie noticed that a group of men were giving him the eye from the other end of the bar. They were a rowdy-looking bunch, scraggly in faded denim—cowpunchers who were most likely from St. Paul or Lee County, he figured.

Davie approached the men, and as his words began to formulate the sentence that would surely incite the rustlers, he felt his heart rate kick up a few notches.

"My pa' always said a look ain't never kill't no one," Davie said, removing his Stetson. "But I have." He set his hat and phone onto the bar.

Onlookers quickly gathered around to back Davie. Then Janice chimed in, and Davie caught a whiff of her perfume before snagging sight of her in his peripheral view. She had worn the same fragrance since high school.

"Reckon you boys best leave while you still have a chance," she told them.

The largest of the men stood up from his stool with a wild look in his eye.

"Know your place, bitch," he said to Janice. "Before—"

Davie punched the cowboy in his throat, then slammed his head down onto the bar.

All hell broke loose.

Davie … The Brawler

Chapter 4

Squirrel, holding a lengthy fuse in one hand, and a stick of dynamite in his other, treaded up through the driveway of Roy McCaffrey's farmhouse. The air was rancid, reeking of slaughtered animals that were days beyond decay. Roy managed his property poorly, and due to blatant neglect, his livestock was succumbing to sticky infections and malnutrition, which has ultimately driven him in debt with the city and more. Roy and his useless wife, Karen owed Squirrel and his brothers $5,000, and he was there to collect.

Through an upstairs window Squirrel saw Roy and Karen's two daughters jumping up and down on a bed. He grinned, because people become mounds of mush when the lives of their children are threatened.

Squirrel dropped the stick of dynamite and kicked it underneath Roy's pickup truck, then headed back down to the dirt road where his car was parked.

Squirrel learned early in life that people would take him lightly if he lightly addressed the situation, so he usually just cut the rope and let the scoundrels fall to their deaths. His ma' once said that pussyfooting was for politicians—that real men don't talk about what they're going to do—they just do it.

While thinking about his mother, a sadness overtook him. She was a hellion, a certified hick with a fiery response to anyone or anything she disagreed with. Squirrel was a lot like his mother—even more so than his father, who single-handedly raised him and his brothers after their mother died of multiple sclerosis in 2007—eighteen years ago. Squirrel was ten years old when his mother passed, and although hurt and full of bitterness, Squirrel was relieved to finally see her suffering end. The muscular tremors and partial paralysis were heart-wrenching.

Unlike his brothers, who all favored their father, Squirrel was skinny and shorter than any of his siblings—facial structure like his mother's, with a lazy eye he had since birth. Even on an inky night like now, with a clouded full moon, he wore sunglasses to obscure a lifelong insecurity.

With a body cluttered in tattoos, a blond mohawk, and several facial piercings, Squirrel was a total badass—and one would be smart to fear him.

Reaching into his pocket for a burner phone he'd purchased for this particular occasion, he dialed Roy's number, then lit the fuse.

Roy answered on the third ring. "Hello?"

Squirrel leaned against the passenger side door of his SRT Hellcat, then said, "So I guess you're answering every other phone number but mine?"

Silence.

At that moment, Squirrel pictured Roy's eyes stretching as wide as fifty-cent piece coins.

"Squirrel?" Roy finally said.

"You know it's me, you fat sumbitch. Now where's our goddamn money?"

"I—I—I need more time."

"Wrong answer."

The pickup truck exploded into the air with a fierce, fiery ball that shattered the windows of the house.

As Squirrel marveled at his destruction, his primary phone was ringing inside the car.

It was his brother, Rock-on, calling.

Squirrel … The Nutcase

Chapter 5

Merle and his best friend Randy were having a drink while engaged in a quiet game of chess. Merle, who always wore a colorful NASCAR cap, studied the board. If it was one thing he had learned in life, it was patience—the level-headed sibling who, unlike the others, had successfully eluded the long arm of the law.

The television was muted, but live rodeos didn't require much sound to convey an event. Cowboys either held their grit or bit the dirt. Logs crackled in the fireplace, projecting a substantial amount of heat throughout the house. The panel walls were the color of elephants blotched with mud—mounted elk heads, stuffed falcons, owls, turtle shells, and dream catchers made up the decor around a plush living room suite that blended perfectly with the bearskin rug—the redneck sense of beauty.

Merle was a family man. He was not prone to sexual dalliance or flirtatious side dealings with any of his female staff members. He loved his wife and children more than God himself—if that meant anything to anyone—because Merle was not much of a believer, but the statement clarified the depth one could imagine he would go for his family. They were who he lived for.

Merle's wife, Freah, was in the kitchen preparing dinner. The heavy aroma of her highly requested shepherd's pie drifted freely, arousing hunger in the little ones upstairs.

Merle moved his castle, then downed a shot of lightning. Randy made the best moonshine in the county, and Merle usually had first dibs on a batch of shinola—he was quite the drinker.

"So, what we gone do about them Lee County boys?" Randy asked Merle.

"I'm not too worried about 'em."

"They're undercutting our prices, and hell, how I see it, you don't walk into a man's house without first wiping your goddamn feet."

Merle thought about Teddy Lee and his outrageous attempts to shut them down, which commonly resulted in a number of idle threats that Merle always responded to with the same tone of words: *"Don't threaten me with a good time, Teddy Lee."*

"If their ice was even worth a damn, I'd agree," Merle said. "But they're selling garbage for a little of nothing." He scoffed. "Buy one, get one free. Lot to Friday. Good product doesn't need any gimmicks, son. And by George, if we ain't got the best shit in the region, Momma June a whore by Sunday, boy."

Randy nodded. "I get that, Merle, I do. But them Lee County boys ain't known for business like you, son. They're stupid-violent."

Merle looked across the table at him. Merle owned the *Ride 'em Cowboy Billiard & Bar*, a hog farm, two marijuana dispensaries, and a popular coffee shop downtown. He was preparing to bow out of the meth game gracefully, but Randy wasn't entirely wrong—Teddy Lee and his little band of inbred degenerates were dumb enough to do something stupid.

Randy continued, "They're retarded, if you ask me. Always wanting to fight and thangs." He moved his knight, then reached for his beer.

Merle, who was a sizable man with a salt-and-pepper beard, was no stranger to hostility—he had busted more than a few heads in his days.

Narrowing his dark brown eyes, Merle said, "Hellfire, Randy. We ain't no pussies ourselves, you know?"

Randy, cheeky like a groundhog with flabby earlobes, gave an exasperated look. “Goddamn, Merle, I know. I’m just saying that, you know, maybe we shouldn’t take them so lightly.”

“If push comes to shove, we’ll shove them bastards so far into the ground folks’ll find ’em in China.” He moved his queen. “Checkmate.”

Randy stared at the board, baffled. “Damn, didn’t see that coming,” he said.

Merle grinned, revealing nicotine-stained teeth. “And if Teddy Lee keeps poking at a bear, neither will he,” he said.

Merle’s phone rang. It was his brother, Rock-on, calling.

Merle … The Thinker

Chapter 6

The football game was intense, down to the wire, and the visiting team, Appalachia, was winning by six points with only a minute remaining on the clock in the fourth quarter. If Norton High doesn't score, this rival match up is in the books.

Norton had the ball on the ten-yard line—ninety yards from sealing a victory. The night air was frosty, but the fans were worked up to the extent that the bold December air was not an issue.

The left side of the field was chanting loudly, pumping their fists, waving flags that promoted team colors as the Norton High cheerleaders turned cartwheels to boost morale.

"Errol! Errol! Errol! Errol! Errol!" they chanted, encouraging Norton's star running back, who had pushed it to the limit tonight.

Errol smiled. This was his high school, and he'd be damned if he allowed Appalachia to come into his house and walk out with his legacy.

The quarterback, Jack Taylor, took position behind the center, dug his cleats into the stiff dirt, then looked to his left, to his right.

Errol, in the backfield, took a deep breath. His younger sister, Cathay, was currently sick with a severe case of pneumonia, so his parents couldn't make the game tonight. Although it was selfish and inconsiderate of him, he openly voiced his disappointment over the phone, which caused a heated exchange. For some reason beyond Errol's knowledge, he had always felt the need to live up to his father's expectations, which were very high. Merle was great at everything he'd ever done—football included—and Errol just wanted his father to be proud of him.

"Down," Jack said. "Saaiid," he dragged the word out. "Hut!"

Jack tossed Errol the ball, and with a tremendous burst of speed, he bolted through an opening that his linemen created for him. An opposing player dove for his legs. Errol leapt into the air to avoid contact, landed, and spun to elude another before stiff-arming Riley Lockett, Appalachia's top defensive player. The left side of the field went ecstatic, yelping, whistling, and howling as Errol tore past the fifty-yard line like a Mac truck.

Appalachia's head coach slammed his cap to the ground. "Goddammit!" he yelled, turning beet red. "Get 'em!"

But Errol was too far gone—there was no stopping the boy at this point. It was just him and the open field.

"Touchdown!" came the commentator's voice through the loudspeaker.

Errol, with a huge smile on his face, looked to the Norton High cheerleaders, and just as he hoped, she was staring at him as she leapt up and down with her pom-poms. Her name was Harley Patterson, and she was by far the prettiest girl in school. The two of them had had their eyes planted on each other for quite some time, and now that she and Derick Becher were officially broken up, Errol planned to make his move on her tonight at Georgie Carlson's house party.

Errol's teammates picked him up into the air in celebration of the touchdown.

Errol … The Star

Chapter 7

Errol walked through the front door of the house party with a bottle of whiskey in his hand. The place was packed, loud, and smoky. Tobacco and marijuana—two of Errol's favorite vices.

"Yee doggy!" Errol yelled over the volume of music and laughter, alerting the room to his entrance.

The room erupted in cheer as other players from the Norton football team trailed into the house with cases of beer tucked under their arms. Appalachia attempted to make the best of the remaining seconds on the clock by throwing a Hail Mary pass that was intercepted by Conor Staples—Norton's top cornerback.

Georgie threw the biggest parties in the hills, and like always, he was seated in the heart of the gathering with his lips wrapped around a meth pipe. Georgie was a senior two times over, but it was rumored around school that he had a great chance of graduating next year with the rest of them.

Events such as beer pong, drunk Uno, and hog wrestling were just a few things taking place inside and outside the house. Twin sisters, Stacy and Tracy Wilcox, were sledding down the steps on pillows, while Bobby Lanceford danced provocatively with a blow-up doll.

"Well, hellfire, son."

"Go, go, go, go, go, go!"

"Uh-uh, move, Sam, get off me!"

"This shit'll put hair on your knuckles, boy."

Came a random dialect over the blare of good ol' country music. Georgie's pet iguana took refuge on a curtain rod, staring down at the confusion curiously.

Errol was greeted generously—pats on his back, hugs, and genuine smiles. His popularity was enormous, and although he was kind, respectful, and just an all-around good guy, it was the free drugs that he normally stole from his parents' bedroom closet that made him *out*—fucking—*standing*!

Georgie spotted Errol and cracked a lopsided grin. "The party has arrived, people," he said, standing up from the sofa to greet his pal.

With a smile, Errol shook Georgie's hand and said, "You missed the game tonight, fucker."

Georgie wagged his finger in Errol's face. "Doesn't mean I ain't heard about you, son. Six touchdowns. That's gotta be some kind of record."

Shrugging, Errol said in a cocky tone, "Something light. Didn't even get worked up too tough."

They laughed.

Then Georgie wiggled his brows and asked him, "What you got for us, buddy?"

"Ice."

Georgie beamed excitedly. "Yes. I'm tired of smoking this bullshit that Jerry scored from his uncle. What else, what else?" He pressed eagerly.

"Some coke and some Roxy's."

Georgie's blue eyes bulged, and he pushed his long blonde hair away from his face with his hand. "Roxy's?" He leapt up and down—ecstatic. "Hell yeah, son!"

Errol laughed, then reached inside his coat pocket for the drugs, saying, "Suboxone too."

Georgie's mouth fell open. He loved the pink pills more than he loved his parents, but with everyone in the area pressing the pills with Fentanyl these days, it was difficult to score some good clean product in Southwest Virginia. Errol was the man, but selling drugs wasn't his thing. He just gave it away at parties, because dreams of playing for the NFL consumed him—not inheriting the throne of his father's criminal empire. It meant nothing to him.

With the drugs in his hand, Georgie turned around and pumped his fist in the air. "Time to go to the moon, son," he shouted.

The crowd belched a wave of excitement. Errol headed down the hallway that led to the kitchen, bypassing a few people who were hugged up—lip-locking. It made him think about Harley Patterson. He wanted her so bad he could taste her.

Errol was tall and tough-looking. He kept his hair short and faded with a rat tail that was normally braided. His signature smile and dimples captured the hearts of the young ladies in school, but it was his impersonal kindness that attracted the masses.

Upon entering the kitchen, Errol locked eyes with Harley. She was sitting on the counter, ground-ruling a drinking game called Circle of Death to a number of newbies. He smiled. So did she. Her long curly strawberry-blonde hair flowed past her delicate face—stopping just short of her waistline, perfectly accommodating her cute, freckled nose and emerald-green eyes. Eyes that said, *"Come to me."*

Errol looked to his right at a table of classmates and saw Harley's ex-boyfriend, Derrick, downing a beer. Derrick had always looked older than any of them, and although Errol had a thin mustache with a patch of hair on his chin, Derrick had him beat—deep-set eyes, receding hairline—the results of a stressful upbringing. Errol and Derrick had never had a problem with each other, but everyone was aware of how Derrick commonly behaved whenever anything pertaining to Harley talking to another guy came up—irate and downright obsessive. But Errol was a long stretch from cowardly, and everyone knew it—Derrick, especially.

Errol set his bottle of whiskey down on the table and walked directly between Harley's legs to plant the biggest kiss in the world on her soft pink lips. Throwing her arms around his neck, she pulled his tongue into her mouth. She tasted of alcohol. He tasted of spearmint. She smelled sweet, perfumey. He smelled of body wash, a masculine odor that she totally agreed with.

"Woo hoo!" hollered a handful of people.

Derrick choked on a gulp of beer. He was completely thrown off by the so-called deceitful act.

"Oh my damn," laughed a girl, blushing.

"Hot damn," said a boy with a huge smile.

"That goddamn Errol. Get 'er done, boy!"

The comments and cheering continued, but Errol and Harley had slipped into la-la land.

There was no longer any room to fight it—they both wanted the likes of the other, and it had never felt so right.

They parted and stared into one another's eyes. Magic, and sparks, sparkled beautifully.

"Wanna go outside?" Errol asked her.

She bit down on her lip, hardly able to contain her excitement. "Yeah, I'd like that."

He helped her down from the counter, then took her by the hand—both purposely avoiding the murderous glare of Derrick. Errol grabbed his bottle of liquor and told Harley, "Get two of them cups for us, baby."

Harley blushed.

Errol led her to the back door. Walking out onto the deck, they spoke to a few people before descending the steps that led to the yard. An incredibly tall bonfire gave the grounds character. The barn was highly active with wildly drunk teens—the mechanical bull would not rest.

Errol and Harley took a seat near the fire. Damn, did that heat feel good.

"Wait, before you shoot your goddamn pecker off, you stupid sumbitch," came a voice from around the side of the house, then a gunshot cracked loudly.

"So, do you normally just walk up and kiss gals on their mouth?" Harley said jokingly.

Errol smiled.

Damn, she loved his smile.

"Not at all," he answered, pouring her a drink.

"So why all of a sudden?"

"Suddenly felt ready."

This intrigued her. She looked up from her cup, saying, "For?"

"Us."

"Hmm. Really? Because you've been staring at me for months. Why now?"

"Oh, so I've been the only one staring, huh?"

"I mean, I looked a few times."

They threw their heads back with laughter, neither aware of Derrick's presence on the deck.

"Well, Derrick, of course," Errol admitted.

"Plus Crystal," he added, mentioning his ex-girlfriend.

"Oh yeah, I did date that asshole, didn't I?"

Taking a swig of liquor, Errol nodded and said, "Sure did, and you oughta seen his face in there just now."

Harley sucked her teeth irritably. "You think that's something, you oughta seen that dickhead's face when I broke up with him. I don't know who the hell raised that boy, but grabbing me the way he did—"

"Yeah, I heard about y'all's fight."

"Oh, it wasn't gonna be no fight. I was gonna cut that punk from asshole to elbow," her expression tightened. "Putting his paws on me like that? Uh-uh. That dog ain't gone hunt."

Errol smiled. Harley was spicy, and he liked a little heat in his women. His mother was a ghost pepper, so it made perfect sense.

Eager to change the subject, Harley asked him, "So, now that you're ready for us, when does *us*, start?"

"Now."

She arched a brow. "Now?"

"And forever."

She liked that.

They kissed deeply, passionately—tongue wrestling. Errol had wanted this girl since the very first day she walked into his biology class a year ago, and now that he finally had her, he had no intention of ever letting her go. High school was a tricky place, full of curious young minds who were all looking to experience adulthood far too early: love, sex, drugs, and money. But Harley was different—she wanted more than the discoveries of everyday life and often spoke in class about foreign cultures and how she wanted to see the world. Errol would follow her to the ends of the earth, that he knew.

Then, strangely, both of their phones rang, and upon looking at their devices, they both said, "It's my pa."

They laughed at the coincidence. Harley's father was calling her on FaceTime, whereas Errol's dad was calling from their landline—Merle doesn't normally keep his cell phone charged, so he added an additional line for his personal chats.

"I have to take this," Harley said, standing up from her chair.

"Yeah, me too."

Harley walked out of earshot, then answered the call. "Hey, Dad."

It was Teddy Lee, and lying next to him on the countertop was his trusty sledgehammer.

"Hey, darling. What you doing?"

"Nothing. Just hanging out with some friends."

"Sounds like a lot of friends."

Harley grinned. "Yeah."

"You still coming down this weekend?" he wanted to know.

Harley was from Lee County, born and raised, but her mother's roots stemmed from Norton, and a year ago, her mom decided to move back home for a fresh start. That had worked out incredibly well for them, considering that her mother had not only held down a job, but she had also remained drug-free. Initially, Harley hated the idea of leaving her friends, house, and everything else she had ever known, but she had come to like Norton—a lot—and now that she was finally with the guy who had occupied her thoughts for months, she really, really liked Norton.

"Yeah, I reckon," Harley said, not exactly enthused with the thought of spending the weekend with her father.

"Well, don't act so excited," Teddy Lee said sarcastically.

"No, it's just—"

He cut her off. "Just what, huh? The weekends are supposed to be our time together, Harley. Your mother and friends get to see you enough."

Harley looked away, ashamed, but managed to speak despite the lump in her throat. "Sorry, Dad. You're right."

The truth was, Harley hardly knew her dad. She was only 1 year old when he went to jail for first-degree murder, and now, here it was, 17 years later, and he was back in her life trying to make up for lost time.

"It's okay, sweetheart. I just wanna see you, is all," Teddy Lee expressed.

Harley looked at Errol. Something was wrong. He appeared deflated, as if all the life had been sucked out of him.

"Dad, I gotta go. I'll see you tomorrow."

Harley ended the call and hurried to Errol's side, saying, "Hey, you okay?"

Errol's eyes were pools of pain.

"Hey?" She urged, her voice as delicate as cotton. "Talk to me. What's wrong?"

"Someone . . ." His voice cracked. "Someone killed my uncle."

Harley's mouth fell open. She couldn't believe her ears. "Oh my God. I'm sorry," she hugged him. "That's horrible."

"I have to go." He sniffed.

Without thought, nor hesitation, Harley said, “Let me grab my coat.”

From the deck, Derrick eyed them evilly. To him, this was an ultimate trespass on Errol’s behalf—punishable by death.

Chapter 8

Merle slammed his foot on the brake, and his Silverado slid to a halt. Floodlights blazed the forest, drawing shadows from the trees and enhancing the fretful visuals of a coroner's van, deputy cruisers, and yellow tape. Merle couldn't believe this shit. Dog Man—his fucking younger brother—dead!

How?

Why?

Who?

Merle took a deep breath. He was shaky, fearful of the details that awaited him. Dog Man and him had always been as tight as thieves, and he couldn't fathom the thought of never speaking to him again. As teenagers, they would walk down to Jixxy Market on Main Street to score a twelve-pack of Pabst Blue Ribbon beer, which was the only brand that Dog Man would ever drink. Then they'd head to the river to cast a few lines into their favorite granny hole, which was usually teeming with striped bass and bluegills. It was at these moments, sitting alongside that muddy riverbank in the scorching sunlight, that they truly confided in each other. Dog Man would often speak about leaving Norton and going to San Antonio, Texas, to join the rodeo. He would tell Merle about all the so-called pretty gals who followed the sport and how he heard that San Antonio had buildings that were as tall as the heavens. But once their pa fell ill to Parkinson's disease and could no longer work, Merle and Dog Man—being the oldest—had to pick up the slack to keep the family afloat. As time progressed, their father's medical expenses became overwhelming, depleting their meager paychecks and eventually cornering them into a hole. With a slew of past-due bills and the city looking to close on the property, Merle considered the unthinkable. His rash decision to peddle crank (meth) was why Dog Man never followed his dream to shine in the Lone Star State. He stuck by Merle's side and became a drug lord instead.

"I can't believe this," Freah said, quietly sobbing. "He was just at the house this morning."

Merle looked over to his wife. He met Freah in the second grade, and he had loved her for an extensively huge portion of his life, but it wasn't until they were in junior high that Dog Man took it upon himself to enlighten Freah of Merle's unwavering crush, which, fortunately for Merle's sake of dignity, aroused Freah's admittance of her personal infatuation with him. Dog Man was responsible for triggering one of the greatest love stories that Freah and Merle had ever witnessed—their own. Freah loved Dog Man like a brother, the brother that she never had in her own sibling—the sibling that Merle and her had killed, long, long ago. Their secrets ran deep, but nowhere near as deep as their loyalty to each other.

Randy spoke from the backseat. "Reckon we know who did this." It was more of a statement than a question. "Everyone knows how close you two were. This is a message."

Merle looked into the rearview mirror. Randy was staring out into the night, his bottom lip stuffed with spit chew. Randy had warned him several times about the wrath of Teddy Lee, but more so about the fire of revenge. Although Teddy Lee and his clan of faithless souls were out to reclaim the glory of power, Teddy Lee had a personal issue against Merle, who at one time had been his best friend.

Merle didn't comment. He took a deep breath, then sucked his teeth, which was a common habit whenever he was thinking. Dog Man was a loner, and he was honorably faithful to Lisette and their five children, so his death could not have been the result of some wildly impractical love triangle. Dog Man found joy in breeding canines and hunting game throughout the Appalachian hills, but High Knob Mountain was not a location that he would even consider. Campers and pathfinders who were in search of breathtaking scenery normally frightened the wildlife, so this particular area would not have interested him in the very least. Meaning that he had been brought up here against his will.

A moment later, they all got out of the truck and were met by the distinctive wailing of tree toads and the trickle of several waterways that embraced the land. Merle wanted to turn back and wake from this God-awful nightmare. With every step he took, he could feel his breathing contract more and more—detesting the smell of nature that reminded him of the last time he joined Dog Man on an excursion up through the Blue Ridge Parkway—buckskin territory.

The family was present, and Squirrel was crowding Sheriff Dougherty's space. The two were immersed in a heated exchange of words.

"Back up!" Dougherty shouted.

"Let me see my brother," Squirrel ordered.

Deputies stood guard, backing the Sheriff while blocking the perimeter. A forensic unit channeled about as a couple of pointer dogs sniffed the grounds for possible leads.

"What can you tell us, James?" Merle said, addressing the Sheriff by his first name.

Dougherty, a towering Black man with short, coarse hair and a handlebar mustache, looked past Squirrel and saw that the level-headed brother had arrived. Lisette hugged Freah, crying hysterically in her friend's grasp.

Dougherty tipped his hat and said respectfully, "Merle."

A gust of shivery wind whipped fiercely throughout the gnarly woods—smacking everyone in their face.

Merle lowered his head and pulled the collar of his coat up around his neck, and once the winds calmed to a hiss, he asked Dougherty again, "What can you tell us?"

"A group of hikers found him tied to a tree back yonder. He'd been beaten pretty badly."

Merle looked to Rock-on and his wife, Savannah. Savannah worked as a 9-1-1 dispatcher, so his guess was that she was the operator who took the call.

"Shot?" Merle asked.

"No."

"Stabbed?"

Dougherty shook his head.

Squirrel, never the subtle one, shouted, "Then what? What the fuck happened?"

"Yeah," Davie added.

The deputies cleared steel from their holsters—Davie and Squirrel put folks on edge. They were unpredictable.

"That's enough," Merle told his brothers.

"This is a crime scene, goddammit. Don't be stupid."

Squirrel and Davie both lowered their heads shamefully. Merle was more so their father than an older brother. He was who they looked to once their pa' passed.

"Now, James, I get that you can't let us pass, but give us something," Merle said.

Freah's cell phone chimed loudly. They must've been near a tower because reception at that elevation was mostly choppy. She reached into her back pocket for her device.

Dougherty sighed. This wasn't easy for him. "His . . ." He shook his head, wishing to vanish into thin air. He hated relating such details as of this.

Freah opened a text message from an anonymous number.

(267) 424-9551: *Ask that sweet old husband of yours about Bobbi Dupree. And oh yeah, their daughter that they had behind your back!*

Dougherty finally said, "His head and face are completely bashed in."

This hit the family like a bolt of lightning, sharp and unrelenting. Rock-on collapsed to his knees, his body shaking as he buried his face in his hands, struggling to choke back sobs. Squirrel's anger burst out of him like a primal force. He punched the nearest tree so hard that the crack of bone against bark echoed through the night. He screamed at the heavens, the sound a mix of agony and fury, as if he could tear the world apart in his grief.

"Without his driver's license, we wouldn't have been able to . . ." Dougherty said, then figured it would be best if he just shut the hell up.

"Mom. Dad."

Merle and Freah both looked over their shoulders and saw their son Errol and some girl running toward them.

Merle's eyes narrowed into suspicious little slits, and before he even thought to stop himself, he said, "What the hell is he doing with her?"

Freah looked at him—her fiery glare was as equally distrustful as his. "Who the hell is she?" she asked him.

"That's Bobbi's daughter, ain't it?" said Savannah, who so happened to look up from consoling her husband.

Freah's expression tightened. She hadn't heard a thing about Bobbi Dupree in over fifteen years—now this? Freah took a deep breath, because now was not the time to act out, but she definitely had some questions for her husband, who was currently looking as though he just swallowed a stink bug.

Errol hugged his father, saying, "I got here as fast as I could, pa'," then he embraced his mother. "What happened?"

No one spoke. Davie kicked a few rocks around on the bumpy dirt road, but it was a humbling moment.

"This is my girlfriend, Harley," Errol told his parents.

Harley waved nervously. "Hey. I'm so sorry for y'all's loss," she said.

Merle simply lowered his head, as did Randy, who knew that this problem would resurface one day.

Freah, a naturally observant person with keen perception, cut her eyes to Randy, because his sudden discomfort conveyed the notion that he knew exactly what was going on—if not the guilty culprit himself. Freah didn't trust Randy, and she had a damn good reason not to.

Chapter 9

Exiting the church, the family and associates of Dog Man either parted into social groups or headed to the parking lot to escape the grounds of grieving. It was a beautiful service: flowery, polished, and color-coded in Dog Man's favorite colors of blue and gray. His wife, Lisette, and their oldest daughter, Becka, spoke wonderfully of him, very heartfelt, driving many people to tears with simple stories that illustrated the love and support of a great man. Merle, Freah, and Rock-on spoke as well, revealing unknown facts about Dog Man, like his love for pottery and birdwatching.

"He could identify a bird by its chirp, and any western starring Clint Eastwood was a bonafide classic if you let 'em tell it," Merle told the room while combating a fistful of tears.

It was 2:00 p.m., and the sky was a depressive gray. A rumble stirred throughout the clouds, and it was Errol who felt the first drop of rain on his hand—a hand that Harley was holding onto.

Everyone could feel the intensive rage fuming throughout the four brothers' pores—murder was in their eyes, in their hearts, in the near future.

"Now that he's laid to rest, it's time," Squirrel said to Merle.

"Yeah," Merle agreed, looking at Errol and Harley. "Round the boys up. Show these sumbitches we ain't to be yanked around with."

Just as Merle lit his cigarette, the sky parted and spit sizable raindrops upon them. Everyone ran to their respective vehicles. Car doors slammed, and engines came to life within the weight of the downpour.

Freah slid behind the wheel of her Rubicon Jeep and immediately proceeded to get some heat circulating from the vents. The sound of the windshield wipers filled the cab as Freah watched Randy and his wife, Colleen, load into his El Camino. Colleen and Freah had been friends since grade school, and if it wasn't for the sake of her, Freah would've thrown Randy to the wolves by now. But first, she must be sure of her claim, because if she was wrong and Merle killed him, Colleen would never forgive her. Colleen was the glue that held Freah together when they were younger. Freah's older brother, Franky, had been sexually abusing her since the early age of five, and her alcoholic parents usually brushed her aside to reach for a bottle of Canadian Mist. Until this very day, Freah despised her parents and avoided them at all cost. Before she had Merle to confide in, Colleen kept her sane and hopeful. So Freah owed her friend the decent courtesy of giving her life partner the benefit of the doubt, but she would get to the bottom of it—she always does.

Merle swung the door open and hopped into the passenger seat. Freah looked at him. He looked at Freah. There was this unspoken thing between them, a soulmate intuition that comes inside the package of true love. They both detected the disruption of peace within each other. Freah had not told him about the anonymous text message that she received last week, but through a few known associates of hers, Freah had gathered enough intel about Bobbi Dupree to piece together the truth entirely. So, until she uncovered the act of deceit, she was not going to excuse her husband of any wrongdoing, but damn, did it hurt like hell—he was her everything.

"You alright?" Merle asked her.

"Yeah," she lied.

Freah pulled out of the parking space. She hated funerals and wanted to put as much distance between her and that church as possible. The idea of death had never bothered her, but people did. After the things that Franky put her through—her very own flesh and blood—Freah frequently thought the worst of most people, and to prevent ever being mistreated and abused again, she normally deflected any purpose for interaction with town folk or social media. People are rotten, and anything rotten needs to be thrown out.

Freah was a homebody, but by no means was she a portly couch potato with more chins than China. That was quite the contrary. Freah was a track star in high school, and up to this very day, she would rise to the crowing of their rooster, Betty, and run ten miles in any direction on their property. Running had always helped her clear her mind of her past—recurring dreams of that bloody knife haunted her to no end. She would never forget the feeling of plunging that blade into Franky's chest over and over again while shouting, "I'm pregnant, you bastard." The feeling of his flesh snagging hold of the serrated edge of the knife, the resistance of retracting the steel, had never escaped her.

Freah was a beautiful mixture; with the sturdy DNA of the Blackfoot Saskatchewan tribe of northern America, her high cheekbones and long black hair accommodated her round face perfectly, but it was her golden-brown eyes that completed the masterpiece. She was 5'9", 150 lbs, and a marvel to look at in a pair of Levi jeans. However, delightful qualities meant nothing to her, because Merle was the only man she had ever desired to be with. And now, some assholes were threatening to take him away from her. She could not allow that to happen. She would die for her husband and kill any rustler who came near him.

"Where to, hon?" Freah asked Merle.

"Reckon a bite wouldn't hurt none."

It seemed as though Freah was always hungry, and this morning she awoke with a taste for a smasher burger and a plate of curly fries.

Freah grinned and said, “Chili’s?”

Merle smiled, because there was only one Chili’s in southwest Virginia, and that was in Wise County, which wasn’t very far, but too damn far for the likes of a goddamn hamburger. But for his wife, he would walk to Wise County barefooted on a bed of shattered glass, so it was no big deal.

“Chili’s it is,” he said.

Freah reached on the dashboard for her bag of barbecue pork rinds, then said to Merle, “Put some Blake Shelton on, hon.”

Chapter 10

Errol and Harley were walking hand in hand to the river. The soles of their cowboy boots made tracks in the mud with a suction cup effect. The storm had passed, but it was still tousled throughout that part of town, as the clouds gracefully bowed out toward the east. Fallen tree branches and debris from decayed plantation homes littered the riverbanks, and the annoying sound of geese closed in on them from every direction. But neither of the two seemed to care about the many aftereffects of the downpour. They just wanted to be alone, and together.

Normally, throughout the warmer months of the year, the river was a huge hangout for the people of Norton. One would see ATVs and pickup trucks racing between staggering barns and decrepit cotton gins as country music blared from parked vehicles that aligned the banks—drinking, drugging, dancing, and fighting. They called it the Four I.N.G.s.

“Hey, you, you cock-sucking sumbitch. I want that there Philly you got with ya’. Fight for her.”

“Well, goddammit, boy. Why didn’t you just say so? Don’t talk me to death.”

That was how it usually began, but Errol had never taken another cowboy’s gal in a pit brawl, but he couldn’t say the same thing about his uncles.

“That gal of yours finer than a pork and bean sandwich, boy. Only thing she’s missing is me,” he heard Davie once say to Carl Dunbar.

“That there fiddler of yours looking mighty tasty in them jeans, son. Reckon I’d take her off your hands tonight and show her the muscles that really count," Squirrel said one time before beating the living shit out of Donnie Tisdale.

Many men had lost teeth, respect, and their women to pit brawls on the banks, and outsiders deemed it an act of complete nonsense. But for the people of Norton, it was just a way of life.

Harley and Errol stopped at an elm tree with broad branches that reached out to the river.

"So you don't ever want to have kids?" Errol asked her.

Brushing a tussle of hair behind her ear, she said with a sigh, "Well, I wouldn't say ever. Just no time soon. Later in life, ya know? Way later." She pulled the hood of her coat over her head and directed her eyes across the river to an old sugar mill. "Like around the year three thousand and four." She chuckled.

Harley had a cute laugh that was almost childlike—a slight snorkel at the hilt of a bubbly series of giggles. Errol had always found it amusing whenever she chortled, but not about this. Having a family of his own one day was a must. Errol had grown into the likeness of his father and had seen the benefits of love through his parents' devotion to each other and their cause. A couple must have a cause, or else stagnation settles into the bones of the relationship.

Errol reached inside his coat pocket for his foldable blade, then said, "Reckon the thought of having a family turns your stomach, then?"

Harley heard it in his voice. He was disappointed. In all seriousness, she looked at him.

"No. No, not at all. I just think it'll make more sense to wait until the right time, is all, ya know? My folks had me and my sis . . ." Harley's words trailed off.

Errol, who was carving bark from the tree, looked over his shoulder at her. She immediately broke eye contact with him.

"You have a sister?" he asked her.

Her reluctance to respond drew suspicion, so again he asked her, but this time more carefully.

"Yeah," she said with a slight nod of confirmation. "I have a twin."

Errol's eyes stretched wide.

"We're nothing alike, though," Harley quickly added. "Like, at all." She shook her head. "It's complicated."

"Where is she?"

Harley shrugged and said with a frown, "Lee County, somewhere."

Errol heard a temperature of hate in her tone and wondered what could possibly cause two twin sisters to fall out to the extent of such a displeasing glare.

"But," she sighed. "As I was saying . . . My mom had us at a young age, and because of that, we were more of a burden than two sweet bundles of joy, ya know? She could barely afford to feed us. It made her do some pretty bad things." She looked away. Thoughts of her past made her sad. "Why force my hand when I don't have to, ya know? No child deserves that."

Errol had never known a day of hardship, but he had friends who were subjectively poor, so he had seen it firsthand—welfare, hand-me-down clothes, subsidized trailer parks with junkers and underfed animals shadowing the property. But no more than the druggies and druggettes obscured the grounds of no hope—failures.

Errol scratched his chin thoughtfully, considering her point of view. Harley was obviously raised on the other side of the tracks, which explained her fiery attitude and rigid demeanor. He liked her even more now—she was different, in a Lainey Wilson, Ella Langley kind of way—dangerously attractive with an alluring bad girl persona, but smart.

Errol nodded agreeably, then said, "Makes a lot of sense."

Harley arched a brow questioningly. "Yeah?"

"Yeah, it's like my pa' always says: Even the high road can lead to the lowest places."

Her foggy expression indicated that she didn't totally grasp the metaphor, so he filled in the blanks for her.

"Money, sex, hell, looks, even. People take routes in search of thrills and personal gains, or whatnot, and it ends up being a wrong turn of events."

Harley smiled. "Goes south."

He smiled. "Real fast."

Errol directed his attention back to the tree, saying over his shoulder, "Reckon we'll just wait, then."

Harley narrowed her eyes. Why would he say that to her? They were only eighteen years old, for Pete's sake. Who talked like this at their age?

"Would you not do that, please?" she said.

"Do what?"

"Make me feel that I'm it for you. You're Errol, for crying out loud. Girls are lining up to be the next queen of Norton."

Errol turned to face her. "But that's just it, Harley. I don't want a queen."

This baffled her. What did he mean by that? What was more prominent than a queen?

"No? Then what do you—"

Errol cut her off. "Want? I want what every longhorn thinks they want, but fall short of getting because they don't want it bad enough."

Now he had her.

"Which is?" she asked.

Errol took hold of her hands and said smoothly, "You, darling."

Speechless.

Harley looked deep into his eyes in search of the truth, and there it was, staring her smack in the face.

"You really don't know, do you?" he said.

"Know what?"

"Your worth?"

Harley felt her heart patter, and an extended pause lingered longer than it should have. She had never thought much of herself. Her family was incapable of labeling feelings, let alone expressing them, so the words 'I love you' or 'You're a great person, Harley' or 'You can be anything you want to be, kid'—nothing of the sort. Harley's grandfather died when she was twelve years old, and she never saw her grandmother with another man. Harley asked her mammaw why, why hadn't she found another man, and Memaw said, "Because I could never love anyone the way I did him." It was that day that Harley learned what true love looked like, and at this precise moment, it looked like Errol.

"I reckon . . . well, I mean . . ." Harley didn't know what to say to that. "It's just . . ."

"Harley, you're special, girl. I mean, beauty is one thing, but you're so much more."

She smiled, blushing like a school gal in a pageant play. There was so much excitement in his voice. Could this really be it? She had wanted this with him since laying eyes on his handsome face, and now here they were, on the stepping stones that led to a path of love. Errol was tender and kind, and he listened without judgment. Fun-loving and charming—nothing like Derick, who was totally obsessed with himself and could care less about starting a family with her. The tantalizing uncertainties of the future excited her.

"Sorry. I get carried away when I talk about you," Errol said. "And that's my point. When you're with a person who makes you silly, makes you wanna be around them all the time, makes you think about a life with them, you're pretty much all in, darling. A wife who's my best friend is what I want," he raised his pinky finger between them, and Harley hooked her pinky around his. "And now that I have you, I'll—"

She said, "Never let me go?"

He grinned. "Only a fool would."

They kissed. Harley's body tingled in places that had never tingled before. Their affection was meaningful and warm. A minty exchange of saliva as they delved into a realm of ecstasy. Harley was all in.

A minute later, they parted, and Harley looked at the tree—it was their initials.

Chapter 11

Days On In

Leanne swallowed his dick like a pro.

Joker moaned as the head of his rod hit the back of her throat, the sensation driving him wild. The rhythmic slurping and slobbing intensified the pleasure, and he could feel his toes curl as she locked eyes with him, the moment somehow in sync with a Kid Rock tune playing in the background.

Pale moonlight poured into the windows of the bedroom, mixing with the glow of lava lamps and the neon buzz of AC/DC posters. At the instance of highballing into the bedroom while tugging at one another's clothing, the couple found no use of the bed, and instead opted to work their way up from the floor.

"Spit on that cock, you fucking slut, "Joker told Leanne.

This was his usual approach, and while Leanne wouldn't call herself a "slut", she liked to be slutted out between the sheets. She did as she was told—spitting, sucking, nibbling the tip, while stroking his shaft with both hands.

***

While standing at the border of some pine trees, Squirrel mapped his approach. Leanne Hollister's double wide trailer sat in the gut of some bleak hills that resembled camel humps—very little light, but he was certain that she owned a dog.

Squirrel and Leanne grew up together, but ran into two completely different circles. She had never truly dated a man from Norton. Leanne liked outsiders, men she deemed different from the so-called yahoos of Norton. So when Davie told them that she was in bed with the White Infidels, Merle put Squirrel on the job. Sure enough, who did he see Leanne with at Trish's dinner? Joker. A top henchman of Teddy Lee's assembly.

So she was just as guilty of Dog Man's murder as the other bastards, and the reaper was there to collect.

Squirrel knelt to unzip his duffel bag: machete, ice pick, brass knuckles, needle-nose pliers, .357 magnum, a stick of dynamite, blackjack, taser, a bottle of acid, and an AR-15. Weaponry of a mad man.

***

"Shit," Joker said quietly.

Leanne felt his dick harden inside her mouth—stiffened to the point of stone. He was on the verge of cumming. With her hand wrapped around the base of his wand, Leanne swirled her tongue over and under his throbbing bell head before driving his cock in and out, out and in, faster and faster, coating it in thick, glistening saliva—stretching her lips around that monster, conquering her prey.

Joker's body locked, then quivered as he exploded inside her mouth. The sensation was overwhelming, and Joker pleaded for her to stop, but Leanne only became more aggressive at his whiny request. She was a man-eater.

Leanne then slowly crawled up to his torso and straddled his chest. Joker could feel the heat of her pussy against his skin, her wetness. With a mouth full of cum, she kissed him, giving him a taste of his own secretion of love. In one swift motion, she slid down his body and onto his dick. She could no longer resist the temptation.

"Damn," she murmured, feeling as though his dick was in her stomach. "Fuck." Her clitoris was erect and hypersensitive.

Joker sat up from his pillow and grabbed Leanne firmly by the ass cheeks, but allowed her to drive the stick. Wrapping her arms around his neck, Leanne drove the Indy 500, speeding up and down and around as her cheeks clapped loudly against his thighs, pussy juice smacking like a wet washcloth against a wall. She dug her nails into the flesh of his back just as their moans mounted to a peak.

***

Squirrel moved along the perimeter of the property with the handle of his machete in his grasp. Pausing to take a whiff of the air, he looked over his shoulder and saw storm clouds rolling in from the north. The smell of rain had come from out of nowhere, just as he would in the following minutes. He had always found it amusing how things could change in the blink of an eye. As a young boy, he would first watch an animal for several clicks before pouncing to capture it. He anticipated the moment when he would change the outcome of their day with torturous methods that rendered them dead in the end.

Southwest Virginia had been getting pounded by rain all week, but the downpour would be conducive to his mission. Mud and slush would destroy his trail through the woods, and beyond.

Squirrel continued, staying within the blotchy patches of the night while eyeing a doghouse a few feet away from a kiddy pool filled with miscellaneous junk.

Then it happened.

A brindled pit bull darted out the doorway of its house with a vicious growl. The tinkling of a chain against gravel, the clouds of cold air that escaped the canine's mouth as his paws pattered with a drumming effect—Squirrel smiled.

The dog leapt for Squirrel's throat with the snarl of a killer. Squirrel quickly sidestepped the attack and swiped the blade of his machete upward, slicing the fucker's throat wide open.

***

Leanne was riding his dick with rhythm. Her swollen pussy lips kissed the base of his hammer as her large, voluptuous breasts began to perspire. The temperature was rising.

Then Joker's eyes shot wide as the face of an intruder appeared behind Leanne.

"Squirrel, no!" Joker screamed.

Squirrel placed the muzzle of his .357 Magnum to Leanne's skull and pulled the trigger. Blood and brain fragments burst from her forehead and smacked Joker in the face with a splat!

Squirrel grabbed Leanne by her shoulder and slung her dead ass into the wall.

"Get up," he told Joker. "Yellow-belly sumbitch," he kicked him. "Move!"

Joker was tall and lanky, with bad, pimply skin and stringy black hair. The words "White Infidel" were tattooed across the shoulders of his bony back, with an upside-down cross that bore a series of claw marks.

Squirrel walked him out the door, and once they reached the living room, Squirrel raised the butt of his gun and clunked Joker on the back of his head. Joker crumpled to the floor like a heap of laundry—out cold.

Then Squirrel kicked him in the mouth and said, "Stupid fuck. You gone wish y'all ain't lay a hand on my brother's head."

Squirrel reached for an oval-shaped Bluetooth speaker that was blaring an annoying rock song and dropped it into a sink of dirty dishwater. The place was a pigsty, and Leanne obviously ate fast food and drank beer quite frequently. Squirrel kicked a pizza box aside, then reached into his back pocket for a pair of handcuffs. He was an impulsive person, and if it were up to him, he would've blown Joker's brains out faster than the word "Go," but Merle ran the show and he wanted answers, which required patience—something Squirrel didn't possess.

After cuffing Joker's hands behind his back and sitting him in a chair, Squirrel looked around the kitchen and spotted what he was in search of: a can of Crisco oil. Squirrel grinned mischievously, and with a filthy spoon, he scooped large quantities of lard into a cast-iron skillet, then turned the stove top knob to 'HIGH.'

Squirrel was one of those people who commonly kept the melody of one of their favorite songs in their head, so as he loaded his meth pipe, he sang. He hadn't slept in days, and the lines were beginning to blur, but he liked confusion.

The lard began to melt, then from out of nowhere, a rat darted across the floor. Squirrel remained as calm as death, eyeing the rodent curiously as it swiped a stale slice of wheat bread from underneath the table. The rat put him in the mind of Teddy Lee, an intruder who was out to take something that didn't belong to him.

A rat bastard.

But Squirrel was an exterminator, and just like the vermin that scurried down the hallway as if it owned the place, Squirrel intended to put fire underneath Teddy Lee's ass. With that thought, he looked into the living room at a red gas can he'd discovered on the porch—burn all unwanted guests.

Squirrel directed his attention to Joker, whose head was hanging over the back of the chair, Adam's apple exposed—his jugular.

Squirrel placed his pipe to his lips and struck the wheel of his lighter. Instantly, upon inhaling smoke, the hairs on his arms stood up, and his endorphins kicked into overdrive.

Exhaling, he said aloud, "Fuck, that's good!"

The oil was now boiling, popping out of the skillet and onto the stove top. Squirrel took another hit of ice, then sat his pipe and lighter down on the counter. It was time to wake this asshole up. Squirrel grabbed an oven mitt, took hold of the handle, careful not to spill its contents, and turned away from the stove to douse the oil into Joker's face.

"Spzzzz!" came the immediate sound of scorched flesh.

Joker's eyes snapped open, and he hollered like a girl on fire.

"Talk, you rot-gut sumbitch!" Squirrel shouted, smacking him hard in his face. "And it best be what I wanna hear, son." He smacked him again, causing patches of skin to skip across the table and onto the floor.

Joker began to ramble like a blubbering fool. The pain was unbearable, but he finally managed to say, "Okay, okay, okay. Fuck. Shit, man."

"Talk!"

"Teddy Lee killed your brother. I had . . ." Joker's words trailed off. He felt faint and had to take a deep breath. "I didn't have anything to do with . . . to do with it," he took another deep breath. His face and throat were on fire, and the burning sensation nearly placed him in a state of shock. "I wasn't even there, man."

"Who? Then who, you dipshit?" Squirrel said, raising his hand to strike him again.

Joker winced and said quickly, "Jim Bob and Cunningham. They beat 'em good."

Squirrel thought about the brutality his brother underwent on top of that goddamn mountain, and a wave of rage surged through his veins. He grabbed Joker by the jowls of his face and squeezed as tightly as he could.

"What's his plan?" Squirrel said through clenched teeth.

"To kill everyone y'all love until one of you coughs up that recipe."

This particular piece of information rocked Squirrel's core. They were not the targets at all. This altercation had just become completely, utterly horrifying, and he had to get word to the others as soon as possible. So, without another word, Squirrel released his hold on him, and reached underneath his shirt for his gun.

Joker's eyes stretched wide. "No, listen, Squirrel, I can help you. I can—"

Squirrel shot him square between the eyes, and his brains emptied out the back of his head.

Moments later, Squirrel walked out the front door with a trail of smoke behind him. Flames crawled throughout the trailer—not a lick of evidence would survive.

Chapter 12

Several feet away from a massive mahogany desk and tiny kitchenette, in a seating area of the motel room, hardcore pornography filled the screen of a sixty-inch television. The puffy-haired woman moaned hungrily as she sucked a big white cock. The room smelled of various components: cum, reefer, and perfume. A tremendously wonderful concoction.

Down on his hands and knees, Rock-on murmured words of pleasure as Maryanne sucked his dick from the back—mimicking the video. Cum seeped from Maryanne's fleshy, cleanly shaved pussy and trickled down through her inner thighs. Her milky-white skin was feverishly hot and damp. Rock-on had always pushed her to her limit.

Following the trail of the video, Maryanne allowed his dick to fall free of her jaws so Rock-on could turn over onto his back. Her saliva drooled from the head of his tool and onto the drab-colored quilt.

Maryanne turned her back to him and lowered herself onto his face to be licked clean. As Rock-on aggressively tongue-kissed her pocket, Maryanne played with her nipples while jiggling her soft, pretty ass to heighten the moment.

Raking her fingers through her short, curly hair, Maryanne bit down on her lip and began tossing her hips in a slow, rhythmic circle—fucking his face. The woman in the video cried her lover's name. Maryanne did, as well. The woman in the video leaned forward to grab hold of her lover's dick, stroking it vigorously. Maryanne did, as well.

"It's coming, daddy," said the lady in the video. Her voice was whiny and husky.

Maryanne closed her eyes. Her pussy and asshole both shrunk and dilated in a spasmodic manner as her heartbeat and breathing became progressively faster. Due to a clitoris press against Rock-on's upper chest, the stimulation was phenomenal. Her body stiffened, but Rock-on remained relentless, his head leaving the floor in rapid succession of tongue-fucking the shit out of her. Her pussy throbbed and spit hot juice and cum all over his mouth, chin, and upper chest.

Without wasting a moment of time, Rock-on took hold of her ass cheeks and pushed her down toward his member, demanding her to ride it as the man on the video did. Reverse cowgirl was his favorite position, but tonight he intended to introduce something new.

Maryanne sat on his dick and felt the pressure in her soul. Rock-on grabbed her by the nape of her neck with a tug.

"Lay back," he instructed.

Maryanne laid back, flat against his torso, and cried out, "Fuck." As numerous sensations tapped her all at once.

With her head resting on his shoulder, Maryanne began to gyrate her hips as Rock-on played with her clitoris—feeling so good it hurt.

The woman in the video was receiving a facial, her mouth gaping open with thick white cum hanging from her nose and chin, and while stroking his pole, the man grunted pleasurably.

Rock-on and Maryanne were caged inside a realm of ecstasy. They knew how to satisfy each other, but what they didn't know was that trouble was on its way.

***

Flying down the highway at 90 mph in the pouring rain, Savannah cried her little blue eyes out. During the time that everyone was still mourning the death of Dog Man and trying to piece together the facts of his murder, her horn-dog of a husband still found the time to cheat. To which Savannah did not deserve his ass to kiss—especially after all that she had given up for the sake of their relationship.

"It's either him or us," her family told her. She was only a junior in high school then, but she loved Rock-on more than she loved herself, so her response to her family was simple: "If y'all can't accept that I love him, then I—"

At that time and moment, just as Savannah was about to conclude her sentence, her aunt Connie threw her to the floor and held her down as her mother beat her senselessly—a feeble attempt to warn her to stay away from Rock-on, but it only pushed her further into his arms. Later that night, once everyone was sound asleep, Savannah packed an overnight bag and snuck out the back door. It was the last time she ever set foot on her parents' property. She moved into Rock-on's family house, where she was embraced wholeheartedly and treated with the utmost respect, but as time passed, she began to miss her father's quirky sense of humor, her mother's homemade possum stew, and chasing rabbits with her sisters throughout their mamaw's prairie in Pennington Gap.

To be disowned by the people who one loves so deeply causes that person to question whether or not they were ever loved at all, and now here she was, three kids and seventy pounds later, feeling unloved by her fucking husband, of all people!

Savannah was a pretty woman, with long curly brown hair and a dazzling white smile, but over the years she had gained a significant amount of weight and noticed that Rock-on no longer looked at her the same—the fire in his eyes had died, and he rarely touched her sexually—killing her on the inside. But she dealt with it for the sake of keeping their household intact. But once she received a phone call tonight from her friend and coworker, Judy, who claimed to have seen Rock-on and that home-wrecking cum bucket, Maryanne Sweeney, at the Gladdison Motel in Midtown—Room 229—Savannah met her breaking point. She could not tolerate the thought of one more whore who was reaping the benefits of her marriage that rightfully belonged to her.

Savannah glanced over in the passenger seat at her 9mm . . . someone was going to die tonight.

***

Rock-on watched his dick disappear into the dark depths of Maryanne's wet asshole, thrusting fiercely, causing her cheeks to ripple like water. He held Maryanne by her shoulders as she met his momentum, looking back at him with a 'fuck me' face, while the milk of her asshole splashed everywhere.

"You fuck that shit. Fuck it," Maryanne said. Her tone was aggressive, but sultry at the same time. "Goddamn that dick. Fuck yeah, fuck yeah," she moaned.

***

The storm had reduced to a drizzle, but Savannah didn't care to turn the wipers down low or trim the high beams. Her exit was coming up, and all she could ponder was her destination.

Savannah didn't bother to signal. Her Toyota Camry flew up the exit ramp with the damp sound of the road underneath the tires. Coming to a stop at a red light, Savannah looked in her side-view mirror. There had been a set of headlights behind her since she left the house—lights with a bluish hue—a dually truck, she guessed, and diesel from the sound of the cylinders.

The light turned green, and Savannah made a left—so did the truck. She reached for her gun, because her inner voice was never wrong—she was being tailed, but by who was the question?

Savannah looked through the passenger-side window at an open field that was undergoing deforestation. Farmers were cutting down trees to create grassland for grazing because the demand for beef had risen dramatically. Clear on the other side of that range was Maple Street, and she could see the orange and white neon light of the Gladdison Motel sign.

Savannah mashed the gas pedal to the floor and cut a hard right. The Camry bumbled onto the field, causing Savannah to hop in her seat and drop her gun onto the floor.

Sure enough.

The truck burst into the field with tremendous speed and rear-ended the Camry, causing the trunk lid to fly open.

Savannah yelped frighteningly but quickly composed herself so as not to lose control of the wheel. Somehow, some way, she had to get her hand on that fucking gun.

The two vehicles raced across the sodden terrain in a hazardous manner, fishtailing, slinging mud pies and clunks of straw sideways and out. Then . . .

***

Rock-on grunted pleasurably and stiffened as the most intense orgasm he had ever encountered overtook him.

Maryanne quickly crawled forward to turn around and catch her blessing—plopping his dick in her mouth, she felt hot cum spurt to the back of her throat as she slipped her middle finger inside his asshole and directed it along its front wall until she felt his prostate—the male G-spot—and her motions proceeded as, finger, suck, finger, suck, finger, suck, finger, finger, finger, suck.

“Damn,” Rock-on whispered on wobbly knees, feeling as though the crushing sensation was going to cause him to topple off the side of the bed.

***

The distinctive ‘*Blaaaaack*!’ of a machine gun ripped through the night, and the rear window shattered. Savannah lowered her head so as not to be shot and felt the front right tire hit something solid that caused the Camry to spin out of control.

Blaaaaack!

The Camry tumbled across Maple Street and crashed through the front office of the Gladdison Motel.

***

A huge destructive disturbance jarred Rock-on from his state of ecstasy, and with Maryanne tight on his heels, he hurried to the window to see what the hell was going on and saw that the front office was ablaze.

"What the hell?" he said, narrowing his eyes for a clearer view.

People were rushing out the doors of their rooms and running to the accident. Norton wasn't a very big town, so to a certain extent, Rock-on pretty much knew everyone in town—the motel clerk particularly. Maverick was a good friend of his.

Rock-on hurriedly pulled on his pants and shirt and bolted out the door barefoot.

The air was brisk, and there was a clutter of shouting down in the parking lot. Rock-on leapt over the rail of some steps and landed on top of a vending machine in a crouch.

"Oh my God, is that Savannah?" said someone, a man's voice. "That's her car, ain't it?"

"Someone help 'em with Maverick," came a woman's tone.

Rock-on's breath caught inside his chest. Did he hear that man correctly? Savannah? His Savannah? He hopped down from the machine and ran with all his might. A sprinkler system kept the fire at bay as several people carried two bodies to safety.

"Savannah!" Rock-on yelled upon spotting her Camry. "Savannah!"

Chapter 13

Sheriff Dougherty pulled onto Maple Street and veered around the rear end of a fire truck before coming to a halt behind a state cruiser. While taking a moment to assess the scene, Dougherty took a deep breath. Eager reporters and nosy spectators were standing at the perimeter of the yellow tape, as several of his deputies, his elder son Patrick included, were questioning possible witnesses. This was their second location tonight. First, they got a call that Leanne Bartley's trailer was on fire, and after firefighters subdued the flames, two charred corpses were discovered. And now this.

Sheriff Dougherty was a barreled-shaped man, 6'4" with large, intimidating hands—older and approaching retirement, which he was anticipating because Norton was getting too crazy for his blood. The opioid and methamphetamine crisis had driven the crime rate through the roof, so Dougherty was up to his elbows with unresolved cases that had no possible leads whatsoever—a headache, to say the least—especially at his age.

Dougherty looked toward the former front office of the Gladdison Motel and shook his head. Maverick Heffernan was reported as D.O.A., and that was truly sad because he was a good man and a terrific father. Dougherty remembered many nights at Hookey's liquor hole on Dublin and Channing, how Maverick would get shitfaced and go on and on about the time ten years ago when he caught a 5-foot catfish in the Holson River. A true tale, but a very stale one at the bar—very.

Patrick and another deputy by the name of Nash approached Dougherty's cruiser. They were both holding handheld notepads and grim expressions. Patrick was a spitting image of Dougherty's heyday, but he was a lot sharper than Dougherty had been—he was a modern-day black Columbo, which was a little inside joke at the department that Patrick found highly amusing.

Dougherty got out of his car and hoisted the waistline of his shorts up over his belly. Cold weather had never bothered him as much as pants did—he hated trousers—always had.

"So what we got, boys?" Dougherty asked them.

"Well, as I told you on the phone," Patrick said, taking a look at his notes as he always did before elaborating his theories. "Maverick's dead."

Dougherty nodded. "And Savannah?"

Nash answered. "Holding on by the grace of God. Shot three times."

"She's banged up pretty bad, pops. They're not expecting her to live."

"God's will, she'll pull right on through, though," Nash added.

Nash was a holy man who joined the department in the gusto of pursuing the greater good, but the only thing he had seen in his three years on the job was the work of the devil.

Patrick pointed across the street and said, "The trail leads to that open range, right over yonder."

Dougherty looked over his shoulder to the field and saw a couple of flashlight beams swaying through the darkness.

"Blake and Sterling are collecting shell casings, track marks, and whatnot. I reckon the chase began on the next street over, maybe before, but as of right now, ya know, the streets are all wet and all, it's dark, we couldn't really make out much."

"We found a gun in Savannah's car," Nash said. "A nine millimeter."

"Did she use it?"

"Nope. Darn thing was still on safety."

Dougherty was thoughtful. He was piecing together theories of his own. Dog Man, Savannah. He didn't believe in coincidences, so there had to be something there that could bring all of this together.

"I done some digging, pops," Patrick said, surveying his notes. "And folks told me that Leanne was dating a man named Clyde Paylor, who goes by—"

Dougherty's eyes narrowed, and he said, "Joker?"

"Yeah, right. You know 'em?"

"Troublemaker," Dougherty said with a tight nod. "Didn't know he was out, though. Boy went down years ago with—"

"Teddy Lee Richardson," Patrick said, flipping a page of his notepad. "Leader of the White Infidels."

Nash arched a brow questioningly. "The biker gang? Jesus, I haven't heard about them in ages."

"My guess is that the second body from the fire is Joker," Patrick offered.

"I'm listening," Dougherty said, wondering where his son was going with this.

"Well, once I heard about Joker's ties to this gang, I called Thelma Jo and asked her to send me everything we had on them."

Thelma Jo was the desk clerk at the department, and although she was as smart and thorough as they come, Dougherty knew that they didn't have much information on the gang—they were labeled inactive.

"And she didn't find much of anything," Patrick continued. "But one valuable fact did jump out at me."

"Which was?"

"Teddy Lee Richardson is home. Released two months ago from the onion."

Red Onion was a level 5 maximum security prison in Wise County that housed the worst of the worst.

"Hmph," Dougherty mumbled as the wheels turned inside his head.

"Are y'all thinking what I'm thinking?" Nash said.

"There's a war brewing in Norton," Patrick said, and Dougherty and Nash nodded agreeably.

"They're taking one another out," Nash figured. "And I bet you a hot dog to a doughnut it's over meth, 'cause that crap is king around here."

With a sigh, Dougherty looked at the reporters and said, "Don't I know it."

More methamphetamine was pushed through that small corner of Virginia than the entire state, spilling over into Tennessee, Kentucky, and North Carolina. It was big business.

Dougherty's phone rang. He reached into his pocket for his flip phone—he didn't recognize the number.

"Sheriff Dougherty, speaking," he answered.

"Sheriff Dougherty. This is Detective Stonebeck of the Abingdon Police Department."

Abingdon, Virginia, was a town just north of Norton—an hour's drive at most and known for its traditional post-war landscape and southern hospitality.

"What can I do for you, detective?" Dougherty said, giving his deputies a look, because such phone calls were not ordinary at all.

"I have a body up here that was ditched on the side of the highway, and his license says that he's a resident of Norton."

"What's his name?"

Dougherty's mouth fell open.

"And he was tortured, that's for sure," Stonebeck said. "Something or another carved in his chest 'bout a recipe'."

"Sweet Mary and Joseph," Dougherty said. "It's about to be a shit storm."

Chapter 14

Merle and Freah rushed through the doors of the emergency room, with Squirrel and Davie trailing behind them. Due to an accident on I-28 that caused a senior citizen traveler's bus to tumble down an embankment and collide into a column of trees, the hospital was chaotic.

"There he is," Freah said, pointing across the room to Rock-on, who was pacing the floor of the waiting room with a worrisome expression on his face.

They all hurried to his side, Merle being the first to embrace his younger brother. Rock-on was tearful and shuttered in Merle's grasp. Rock-on, although a heartlessly promiscuous hund dow, was a tender soul whose sexual behavior had compromised the clarity of his humble nature that Merle and the others knew existed inside the reversed party animal that everyone saw him as.

"How's Savannah?" Davie asked.

Rock-on wiped his nose with the back of his hand before responding. "Not too good. She's in surgery, but . . ." he shook his head. "This is all my fault. I should've been at home and not—"

"This is only one person's fault, boy. And I tend to string his ass up by his balls and cut 'em down a size," Merle said with a sneer.

Rock-on's expression fogged. What did Merle know? And it was at that point that Squirrel chimed in to reveal what he had learned from Joker. Rock-on listened intently and without interruption. He was eaten up with guilt, but as vengeful as an agitated boar. He wanted the head of the fucker who was responsible for shooting his wife on a spit by sunrise.

Yet again, Rock-on's lifelong struggle to identify with his feelings had caused him to step out on his wife, who was his everything, and now, because he wasn't present to protect her, she was lying underneath a scalpel, fighting for her life. It was safe to say that his internal environment was ravaged by pain. Savannah didn't always give him what he needed, which was 100%—more than he had ever given in return. "Until death do us part" was a pledge, and not some flimsy doohickey term of false endearment, as Rock-on had considered it to be. Tricks are for kids, and at the moment, he felt like the biggest clown there is. So, as far as self-promises go, he vowed to never cheat on Savannah again if she made it through this dire ordeal successfully.

"That half-cocked sumbitch trying to squeeze Dog Man's mixture clean outta us," Davie said once Squirrel concluded.

Merle nodded grimly. "Reckon it'll work too if we don't find this bastard soon. And I mean like, right now, son," he said.

"How are we gone protect everyone while running these scoundrels down?" Rock-on wanted to know.

Merle, Davie, and Squirrel all shot each other a look, because Rock-on was not a violent man, and this murky situation demanded blood.

"What . . . what is it?" Rock-on asked, noticing the change in their demeanors.

"Lisette and Becka have your youngins," Merle told him. "They're getting everyone down to Kingsport to my warehouse, back yonder, on—"

"The river," Rock-on said, remembering when Merle first bought the piece of property a few years back. "That's smart. Reckon a soul don't know about that place."

Kingsport, Tennessee, was 40 minutes south of Norton—known for a chemical plant that employed the majority of the people of residence and slightly beyond. A town that was full of character and diversity—large enough to lie low and keep watch of what's to come in certain instances.

Lisette and Dog Man were nurturing parents who did a bang-up job raising Becka and their following four children, so Rock-on agreed that Becka and Lisette were the perfect nominees to watch after his girls until they killed Teddy Lee.

"We think you should stay put," Squirrel said, taking the lower route of just outwardly telling Rock-on how they felt. "You know, by Savannah. This ain't gone be that type of rodeo, son."

This angered Rock-on. There was no way in hell that he was going to allow his brothers to slight him of his portion of revenge—First, Dog Man; then Savannah—Fuck that, no way.

"To hell with that, I'm going," he said tightly, meaning every syllable.

Freah stepped away to place a phone call. They hadn't been able to get a hold of Errol, and although Merle had reassured her that their son was very well capable of taking care of himself if trouble were to arise, but Freah wasn't as certain of that as Merle was. Sure, Errol could shoot a gun and was nearly as strong as an ox, but he was not some ruthless cow puncher with a knack for violence. He was in high school, for crying out loud. But just as Freah prepared to dial Errol's number, she saw Randy and Colleen walk through the doors, and she suddenly felt as though she was thrown inside a gunny sack with a viper. Her mind raced back to that alarming moment when she first drew suspicion of Randy . . .

3 Weeks Ago

Not only was it Thanksgiving, but it was also Dog Man's 34th birthday, and the family was gathering at the *Ride 'em Cowboy Billiard & Bar* to celebrate his birthday in style.

Aunt Bella and her alky of a husband arrived, and he cut a beeline directly to the bar. Cousin Dawn and Earl James were bickering over politics, as usual, but otherwise, the festivities were underway.

A towering chocolate cake, shaped like a wild bronco, centered the banquette table, which was filled with various entrees and dishes, such as fried turkey wings, rabbit stew, deer burgers, pickled squash, pulled pork, yams, and much more. The room smelled delicious but appeared much tastier in decor, with gold and black balloons that matched the chairs and tablecloths, a cool light sequence of red, purple, and green, along with an all-girl band who sang a number of country songs while folks square-danced.

"Hot damn, boy. Who sent you?" Uncle Jed slurred with laughter as cousin Pete drank him under the table in an honest man's game of 'Moon Down,' which consisted of downing shots of moonshine until one taps out.

An actor who was hired to attend the function, dressed as a turkey, was standing on top of a pool table, humping the air while wearing a yellow t-shirt that read, 'Happy Birthday To The Biggest Turkey I Know,' with Dog Man's face embellished in rhinestones.

"Shake a leg, darling," Rock-on shouted, rooting for Savannah as she danced the hoedown alongside Freah.

With a broad smile, Savannah blew him a kiss. She loved dancing more than anything. Then the band ended a great song with a break announcement.

Dog Man slapped his knee and said, "Gee, doggy. I still got it, I tell ya."

Lisette laughed and told him, "Yeah, still got a problem staying on beat."

Becka laughed, but it was Jaxon who spoke. "They're just joshing, pa'. You tore it up out there."

"Thank ya, boy," Dog Man said, patting his son on the back. "It takes guts to dance as a man."

Squirrel made fun of his brother behind his back, walking as though he was a decrepit old timer, and Dog Man whirled around and caught him in the act.

"You goddamn turncoat," Dog Man said, chasing his little brother across the floor. "I'll get you yet."

Freah and Merle laughed, then Freah said, "Gotta pee, hon," before kissing Merle on the mouth. "Be right back."

Freah made her way to the rear of the room, passing Errol and Davie, who were arm wrestling. She shot her middle child a look—she was stuffing her chubby little face with pecan pie.

Turning down a hallway, Freah saw Randy talking on his phone. His back was to her, and he was flailing his hand angrily as he spoke.

"Shut up and listen, will ya! Damn Merle. I will be the next king."

Freah's mouth fell open, but she quickly backpedaled before getting made. Did she hear him correctly? The next king?

***

Present Day

The day Randy said he was the next king had been etched in Freah's mind ever since. The thought of it sent shivers down her spine, as though something ominous was going to happen to a loved one of hers sometime.

Her heart was already racing as she began to feel the weight of something off in the air, a sense that she couldn't shake. She felt the hairs on her neck prickle, the hairs at the back of her head tingling with an unshakable discomfort.

The room suddenly seemed to shrink around her, even though she was in the presence of her husband, Merle.

She dialed Errol's number again, holding her breath. Still no answer. Her stomach churned, unease creeping up her spine.

"Freah?" Merle's voice called out. "Is everything okay?"

Freah swallowed, forcing herself to focus. She could hear her pulse in her ears. “No. I can’t get a hold of Errol. He’s not answering his phone.”

“Did you try Georgie? He could be over there, you know?”

Freah nodded, though the unease in her gut deepened.

“Yeah. Said he hasn’t seen ’em since earlier.”

Suddenly, a knock came at the door, and Freah’s chest tightened as she answered it. Sheriff Dougherty stood there. His eyes met hers. They were darker than usual, something unsettling behind them. He removed his hat slowly, tightening his lips.

Freah's heart stopped. That look—the way he held his hat, the way he didn’t immediately speak—it was like a signal, the one her gut had been warning her about all night.

“Folks,” Dougherty said after Freah let him in and shut the door, his voice quieter than usual.

Freah’s hands went cold as the space around her seemed to shrink. She felt suddenly lightheaded, the kind of dizzy that comes before a bad fall.

Merle looked up. “What is it, James?”

Dougherty sighed sadly, and Freah felt a knot tighten in her stomach. She didn’t need to hear the words. She already knew.

“I sure hate being the bearer of bad news, friend,” he said, his voice gravelly, thick with something more than just duty.

“Oh no,” Freah muttered, shaking her head. “What now?”

She could already feel the weight of the impending bad news pressing on her chest, suffocating her. Her breath hitched as her mind raced, trying to process what was coming.

The world seemed to hold its breath as she did.

Freah began to hyperventilate, and Merle took her hand just as she said in a shaky voice, “Just say it, Sheriff, dammit.”

Chapter 15

The city of Ashville, North Carolina was a huge contrast compared to Norton—in size, economy, mobility, and of course, crime. But Teddy Lee could survive and thrive throughout any environment, because lions recognize lions and wolves know the trail of the pack.

Nested in the seat of his Harley-Davidson Fat Glide, Teddy Lee led a gang of his men down the long stretch of Patton Avenue while taking in the glittery skyline of downtown in the distance. Teddy Lee was never much for the city life; it was just way too busy for the likes of him. He preferred the simple things such as idyllic views of verdant hills and lush pastures that smelled of honeysuckles and unpolluted air, good wholesome quality of untouched soil and truculent channels of spring water to drink. City folks stayed too riled up to appreciate the wonders of nature, but he wouldn't have it any other way. Plus, ever since that heartbreaking day that Merle and Bobbi did the unthinkable behind his back, he rather kept to himself and away from society itself—accepting people and the world for what they are—pieces of shit.

Teddy Lee pulled to a halt at a red light. Patton Avenue was packed with the likes of younger folks who were cruising the strip in supped-up cars on large shiny rims, crotch rockets and 3-wheel Slingshots. Blaring horns and overly loud bass conquered the proximity as congregations of people filled into the parking lots of fast food restaurants and various other businesses.

Teddy Lee looked at a traffic cam, then to his watch, making a mental note of the time, because there were two reasons that Teddy Lee and his boys made that two-hour ride to Ashville tonight: one, his supplier lived in a small town on the outskirts, but owned a bar in the city, where they were actually en route to, and secondly, an alibi. If for some strange reason the murders of Savannah and the boy somehow led back to him, the traffic cams throughout the city would omit any wrongdoing on his behalf. He was there to purchase a few kilos of Ice while placing distance between himself and the hits—killing two birds with one stone.

Teddy Lee looked inside the car of four young men who were bobbing their heads to hip hop and smoking reefer. A potent strain that nearly prompted him to say, "How much for a quarter ounce of that there?" But he refrained from speaking, and instead pulled off from the light and made a right-hand turn through the intersection.

Teddy Lee's younger years were a lot more complex than the youth today. He experienced several *don'ts* from his parents, but somehow became exactly who they were—particularly his father, who was a class-A fuck-up, and at one point a pill junkie like his worthless mother. He couldn't change his parents into the warm, loving people that he yearned for as a child, and eventually their long-term influence took hold of him. He started off doing little small devious things around the house with his two younger brothers, but by the time he was 15 years old and working his very first job at a local pizza parlor, Teddy Lee had become a person who began to feel more alive in the midst of confusion—driving him to do such things as masturbating on the pizzas and spitting in customers' colas—anything to throw normalcy off-kilt, he would do it.

But it was the betrayal of Merle and Bobbi that turned his heart to ash. Her pregnancy was just a form of overkill, and as much as he loved Herley, deep down he knew that she wasn't his to claim, but he always has, always will—that will never change. But damn, did it hurt.

Teddy Lee and his boys sped to the summit of Burton Street and embarked on Haywood Road with the growl of V-twin engines. Their destination was a biker bar on the French Broad called *Pure Blood*—a rowdy establishment that commonly required the presence of the APD by closing.

The wind felt good beneath his wings, vigorous in his lungs—this was freedom, and he'll die before he goes back to prison . . . kill before taken back down that dark road. Teddy Lee was only afraid of one thing; and that was himself.

Moments later, the gang arrived at the bar, parking haphazardly on the side of the street with no concern of tickets or tow zones. Muffled bass escaped the two-story brick building and a number of hardcases were standing at the door.

Raising his seat, Teddy Lee grabbed a small duffel bag of cash and tossed it to Jim Bob, telling him, "I gotta make a call. Don't let Tank short us one measly goddamn gram, ya' hear?"

Jim Bob nodded.

Teddy Lee watched his men enter the bar, then reached inside his pocket for a throwaway phone, and dialed Freah's number. It was time that they spoke.

Teddy Lee walked across the parking lot and to the edge of the French Broad River. Silver moonlight danced with the ripple of the wide expansion. As young bucks, he and his brothers used to swim and frolic in a similar body of water in Lee County. Damn how he missed them, and if he thought for one second that he could successfully break into Wallens Ridge Penitentiary and strangle the son of a bitches who killed them, he would at the drop of a hat. This bike club that his father created has cost them everything, and then some.

Freah answered on the fourth ring, saying, "Who the hell is this?"

Teddy Lee grinned. He heard the pain in her voice and imagined the tears in her eyes. His men must've achieved their agenda and executed both Errol and Savannah. Checkmate.

“Reckon I’ve made my point,” he said. “And until my demands are met ya’ll will—”

“Fuck you, you goddamn pussy,” Freah snapped. “We’re gonna find your yellow belly ass, and fry you!”

Teddy Lee chuckled.

“Give me the phone, give me the phone!” he heard Merle say in the background.

“You sumbitch, you think you gone get away with killing my nephew . . .”

Merle’s violent rant progressed, but Teddy Lee was no longer listening to him, and with a crinkled brow he questioned whether or not he heard Merle correctly.

Nephew?

Grumbling a complaint, Teddy Lee slung the phone in the river.

Them dummies killed the wrong boy.

Chapter 16

Errol pulled into the gravel lot of his dad's bar and drove to the rear of the building. Looking over to the passenger seat at Harley, he sang the last bit of *Dance With You* by Brett Young with her. Damn, was she sexy in her black Stetson and Ray-Ban eyeglasses. Her long, curly strawberry blonde hair flowing slightly beyond her ample C-cups, them luscious pink lips of hers called out to him—daring to be kissed. She was it for him.

Another song from Harley's playlist eased from the speakers of the truck, and she continued to sing. She was always in good spirits, and it was highly contagious—so much to the extent that he had his phone setting placed on *Do Not Disturb*. He just wanted to remain immersed in her world without any interruptions.

Then her phone rang, and he saw her disposition quickly change.

"What. What's wrong?" he asked her while slowing down to park near the back door.

"It's my sister," she said, sucking her teeth irritably.

Feeling as though he should give her a little space to talk, he said, "Alright. I'll be inside," then kissed her softly on her lips.

"What the hell do you want, Holly?" was how she answered the call once Errol was out of earshot.

"Where are you?" Holly asked her in a demanding tone of voice.

Harley's expression turned sour, as if suddenly catching a whiff of some dirty laundry. "Why?"

"Because Derick is worried sick about you. Says you're running around with some drug-dealing mo—"

"He's not a fucking drug dealer, you idiot, and I won't have you talk about him that way, hear?"

"You're so stupid, Harley. Going down the same road as Mom did, and look what that got her."

"You, that's what it got her."

Holly scoffed. "Yeah, and we all know that I ain't shit but a worthless spo—"

"Stop it. I told you 'bout talk like that, didn't I?"

"That's easy for you to say. You ain't the one who had to go through . . ." Her words trailed off—it was a touchy subject.

Harley sighed, because Holly has always treated her with contempt, as if it was her fault that people didn't openly accept her when they were children. Kids would call her names and make her cry—adults shunned her because she wasn't normal in comparison to what they consider normal in Lee County.

"You weren't born like this," Holly said quietly.

"We were born together."

"Yeah, but you know what I mean, Harley. Don't be dumb."

Holly was a dark soul—an extremely depressive person who has needed lapses of therapy periodically throughout her life, and was diagnosed with what psychologists call *Radical Acceptance*, which, when it was initially explained to Holly, she was told: "Some problems can't be solved and it can be difficult to accept things that are unfair. Radical acceptance is about accepting life as it is, rather than how we wish it to be."

At eighteen years old, Holly still has not accepted life as it is, and constantly yearns for validation while eagerly set to prove by all means that she belongs.

Holly wants Harley's life—her circle of friends, her freedom to be herself—and all Harley has ever wanted was a sister.

"And why are you talking to Derick for, anyway?" Harley asked her.

"I like 'em, he's cool."

Harley made a face. "Yeah, whatever. I gotta go."

"Harl—"

Harley hung up on her. Conversations with Holly were exhausting, and she normally had to mentally prepare herself before indulging in a verbal exchange of any degree.

Harley got out the truck and entered the building just as a strong gust of wind attempted to overtake her.

The kitchen was spotless, a fortress of stainless steel and classic brick ovens.

"Sneaking through the back, are we?" Harley said with a smile.

"Place closed tonight, sugar. It's just us," Errol said, turning a knob on a fryer, then the flat grill. "Everything okay?"

Harley rolled her eyes. "Fucking Derick, man," she shook her head. "He told my sister I'm dating a drug dealer."

Errol was insulted, because the last thing he wanted was Harley's family viewing him in a negative light.

"You're kidding, right?" he said in a tight tone, with an even tighter expression.

Harley said slowly, "Nope." Then, "We should kick his ass."

"Darn tootin' we should. First thang tomorrow."

Her green eyes lit up as the thought of kicking her ex-boyfriend's scrawny ass really resonated.

"Yeah," she said, raising her hand for a high five.

Errol smiled, because he was not about to let the likes of Derick Finnley ruin their night. Harley was his now.

He bypassed the high five and smacked her on her ass instead.

"Ooh," she said playfully, then hopped up onto the counter. "So, you're gonna cook for Momma?"

"Well, I reckon you can say that, but no."

This confused her. "No?"

"No. See, men are always cooking for gals, and gals are always cooking for men."

She gave him a goofy look. "Uh, duh—"

Errol held out a finger, wagging it, saying, "Not so fast, missy, because even when they do decide to make a meal together, it's within the guidelines of family culture, or what have you."

"My Mammaw made the best chili you've ever—"

He cut her off, smiling, enjoying the good nature of it all. "No way, Jose. I won't be eating Mammaw's famous chili tonight. One day, but—"

Harley laughed and finished his sentence. "Not today."

"Right. Today we're gonna create our own, never-heard-of, Errol and Harley's hoorah."

She beamed. "Oh." She stretched the word.

"Yeah." So did he.

Now a high five.

"What are we gone make?" Harley wanted to know.

Errol rubbed his palms together. "A drink, first. Turn that oven on. I'll be right back."

Errol pushed through a door that led to the public sector to raid the bar. He returned a moment later with a bottle of honey-flavored whiskey and two glasses of ice.

Harley had music playing from her phone, and with her hat, jacket, and sunglasses removed and placed carelessly on the counter, Errol saw that she had gotten comfortable—perfect. He poured him and his favorite gal a drink.

"Follow me, lady," he said, leading her to the walk-in freezer. "Grab whatever you'd like to eat, darlin'," he told her. "And I'll do the same."

"Sounds simple enough."

Harley chose fish filet and chicken wings—two of her favorites—and Errol took to ribeye steaks and ground beef.

Harley chuckled. “Don’t none of this go together.”

Errol shrugged. “Maybe it does. Just have to put our heads together and come up with a hoorah.”

“Hoorah,” she echoed, placing the food on the counter. “With what exactly for the sides?”

“Fries. Okra, maybe.”

Harley made a face. “Uh, yuck.”

He laughed. “Or not.”

Then an idea struck her. “Ooh. What if we deep-fried the steaks?”

He arched a brow. “Like cut ’em up and—”

“Yeah.”

“With some Italian seasoning.”

“Yeah. And garlic. I love garlic.”

“And beer batter,” he said.

Her eyes bulged. “With a bourbon glaze.”

“I like it.”

They laughed.

The couple got to work, trying this and trying that, laughing—throwing tomato bites and lettuce at one another. *Lady Wrangler* by Shaboozey played from Harley’s phone. They danced with the aroma of caramelized onions and spicy chorizo in the air. Harley’s Levis were snug as a glove, and Errol eyed her heart-shaped ass lustfully.

“Good gracious a life,” he said.

“Ain’t nothing gracious about these hips, sweetheart,” she teased. “You best hold on.”

The grease inside the fryer bubbled and popped as crispy sweet potato chips surfaced. Harley swiped her finger in a cake bowl and gave Errol a taste of their concoction—brownie and strawberry cake mixed with walnuts. Errol sucked on her finger slowly while staring into her eyes.

“I’m not wearing any panties,” she said, before biting down on her lips.

Errol grabbed her by her ass cheeks to pick her up and sit her on the counter.

Harley ripped her shirt open, and buttons flew every which way.

“Take me,” she told him in a syrupy tone of voice. “Now.”

Chapter 17

Year 2006

Ever since Freah was five years old, sleep had never come easily—not when her older brother Franky was lurking throughout the house, that is. But of all the nights that she lay awake and struggled not to close her eyes, tonight, at the worst time, she was slipping in and out.

Moonlight poured through her bedroom windows, casting shadows of tree branches on the floor and walls—a windy night with wistful howls that disrupted the shutters.

Lying on her side underneath her favorite peach and green quilt, Freah stared into the darkness of her closet—she could hear him breathing at times of stillness, feel his eyes upon her. Then, against her will, she drifted to sleep.

Minutes had passed, and Freah was dreaming about hiking the Cherokee trails when the rusty hinges of her bedroom door cut into her sleep. Freah's eyes snapped wide. Dim light from the hallway crept across the scarred floorboards. A soiled white Converse sneaker crossed the threshold.

It was him—Franky.

Franky was a tall boy—shabby, smelly, and just downright ugly. He was no stranger to this particular intrusion, so he moved quietly, stepping over or around any weak floorboards and away from direct moonlight.

Freah quickly closed her eyes. She smelled alcohol, and . . . and yes, urine—the bastard was pissy drunk. Mountain Whiskey, their parents' brand. He was following suit to a long line of alcoholism. Freah wanted to do nothing more than kick his sick-minded ass in his balls and spit on him, but just as any other time that Franky had entered her room, she froze.

Franky placed his hand on her shoulder and said, "Daddy's home."

Freah imagined him grinning like the cat who ate the canary, slightly revealing unhealthy teeth.

She heard him undo his pants, and her body tensed up. She quickly searched her mind for a happy place—her Aunt Rose and Uncle Charlie's house in Glade Springs. Running along the lip of the curvy creek, turning stones, seeking crawdads and lizards. Eating snake berries with a pinch of sugar thrown across them—making a mess of herself.

Freah felt the tip of his soft penis touch her lips.

"Open wide, you bitch," Franky slurred.

Freah's eyes popped open, and she did exactly as he instructed her to do—and bit down onto his dick with all of her might.

Franky yelped painfully, but before he could react, Merle charged from out of the closet and yanked his ass into a yoke that put him on his tiptoes. Freah severed his dick from its base, spat it to the floor, then rose from under her quilt with a knife.

Plunging the blade into the center of Franky's chest, Freah shouted, "I'm pregnant, you bastard!"

Again and again, she repeatedly stabbed the fucker as hurtful memories of his abuse flooded her heart with malicious intent.

"I'm pregnant, you bastard."

"I'm pregnant, you bastard."

"I'm pregnant, you bastard."

"Freah!" Merle shouted, snapping her out of her murderous frenzy. "He's dead."

Freah's chest heaved up and down, and she was as jittery as a war veteran with Parkinson's disease.

Merle slung Franky's body to the floor to attend to Freah. She was his main concern.

"Sweetie, you alright?" he asked her, taking hold of her.

Freah nodded, then shook her head. Nodded. Shook. Lost. Scared. Relieved. Elated. Free!

"Get it together, baby. We gotta get him outta here," he told her. "Take a deep breath."

Freah closed her eyes and did as he told her, calming her heartbeat, taking air into her lungs slowly, counting one Mississippi, two Mississippi, three . . .

Moments in, they were heading down the hallway with Franky's body. Time was of the essence. Freah's parents were passed out at the kitchen table, drunk beyond measure—but could awake at any instance and catch them in the act.

Once they were outside, the icy wind felt good against their hot flesh. Luckily, Franky was a frail little something, otherwise the dead weight would've really complicated things. While carefully descending the steps of the porch, a car slowly emerged from the darkness and met them halfway up the driveway.

It was Freah's best friend, Colleen.

"Pop the trunk," Merle told Colleen.

Freah and Merle tossed that no-good bastard into the rear end of the car, then quietly loaded inside the vehicle.

"Where to?" Colleen asked. She was nervous, eyes darting every which way.

From the back seat, Merle said, "Head out toward old man Carson's place. I know the perfect place."

Cold Case 2006–2025
Norton, Virginia

Freah escaped the confines of her unwanted memory and looked back to her phone. She had received yet another anonymous message from God knows who, and it reminded her that Errol belonged to another man—Franky.

And so the message read:

(267) 552-8341: *Here bitch. Take this pic of Merle's daughter and shove it up your cunt. Her name's Holly.*

An image of a teenage girl followed, and through close observation of the picture, Freah didn't see any resemblance between Merle and Holly, but she did look just like someone else in the family.

Hmm?

Freah was seated in the back seat of the truck beside Colleen, who was staring out her window into the night as they entered the town of Duffield. Squirrel and Davie were trailing close behind.

"A pastor?" Randy said, looking over to the passenger seat at Merle. "T-Bass. He's a pastor now?"

Merle, smoking a cigarette, said, "For a while now. Yeah."

T-Bass was one of Teddy Lee's old running partners, and Merle figured that if there was anyone who possibly knew Teddy Lee's whereabouts, it would be T-Bass.

Teddy Lee killed Jaxon, and nearly wiped Savannah off the table with his murderous tactics. But on top of all of that, Errol was missing, and they didn't have a clue where to start. Sheriff Dougherty attempted to ping Errol's phone, only to discover that the department's system had been compromised by a technical issue that arose earlier tonight—another dead end.

Freah and Lisette had always been fairly close, so Merle thought it would be best if she was the one who called her to inform her of Jaxon's death—Dog Man and Lisette's only son.

The pain that Lisette conveyed over the phone was heart-shattering, and Freah couldn't imagine such agony upon her own doorstep. She looked back to the picture of Holly. Errol was not Merle's biological son, but he raised him as his own, and no one besides Colleen knew otherwise. Was it fair? No. Was it her fault? No. But Freah sure as hell felt as though she'd cheated Merle out of a fair handshake.

And now there's Holly.

Jeez Louise.

Randy turned onto Michigan Avenue and pulled over to the side of the road to park. Saint Lutheran Church was down at the opposite end of the street. It wasn't a very large establishment—an A-framed building with an arched doorway and stained-glass windows, white vinyl siding, and dry shrubs that aligned the walkway. But the church was of no immediate interest to them, because sources had informed Merle that T-Bass owned and lived in the yellow duplex house directly across the street from Saint Lutheran, and at this time of night, he was most likely settled in.

Squirrel parked behind Randy's pickup truck, and seconds later, Davie and he got out of the Hellcat and saddled up at Merle's window to discuss their point of entry. The air smelled funky, most likely the result of a nearby paper mill, but it was enough to make one gag—both Freah and Colleen covered their nose and mouth with their hand.

"Reckon the bastard's holed up in there. Looks like every light in the house is on," Squirrel said.

"Sumbitch must be afraid of the dark," Davie added.

"Or he's not alone," Freah assumed, quickly placing her hand back over her face.

Merle shook his head, telling them, "He's always been the busy sort. Moves around like an ant, that man."

"Alright. So what's the plan?" Randy asked.

Squirrel took it upon himself to respond.

"Imma kick the goddamn door down and shoot the sumbitch."

To his annoyance, Merle just simply said, "No."

"Kick the door down and beat shit down his leg," Davie offered, figuring his plan was more logical than Squirrel's.

Merle's expression tightened. His brothers were knuckleheads, and this was not a time for irrational stupidity—not when his fucking son's life was on the line.

"No," Merle said, in all seriousness.

"Maybe you two should just stay out here, because by George, if you two fuck me outta finding my boy, it's gon' get dark real quick and real fast, ya hear?"

Squirrel put his hands up, surrendering.

"Hey, it's your call, big bro. But if this sidewinder don't tell us where they holdin' Errol, Imma clean his whistle, son."

Merle hadn't heard a word Squirrel just said—ignorance normally fell short of registering a formal application in his brain. Merle instead evaluated the neighborhood, taking in the middle-class diversity, petite trees, fine lawns, and narrow alleys—a historic district.

"So what's next?" Randy wanted to know.

Merle looked at him and said, "We're gonna walk right through the front door."

Randy wrinkled a brow. "Say again?"

"Look around. Half of these folks ain't even got curtains up, or their porch lights on. Wholesome folks like these ain't locking their doors never comes to mind."

"That's true," said Colleen. "People move here to retire. You know, to get away from it all. My great aunt Cybil used to live here."

Merle looked over his shoulder at Freah and told her, "Sweetheart, bring that pouch I gave you."

Freah reached down in between her feet for her purse. Merle had swiped a small medical sack from the hospital tonight, but Freah had no idea why he would do such a thing. She figured it was best not to ask. Merle was not a man to question, and she had enough faith in him to follow his lead.

"Uh, I think Imma sit this out," Colleen said in an uncertain manner. "I wouldn't look good in stripes."

This pissed Squirrel off.

"Talk about jinxin' some goddamn one."

Colleen was afraid of Squirrel, so she quickly stammered, "No, sorry. I—I—I didn't—didn't mean . . . it came out wrong."

"Just like you did, 'cause you should've come out your mama's ass instead."

"Hey, dammit!" Randy snapped, coming to his wife's defense.

"Hey what?" Squirrel said with a grit. "Hell you gon' do, boy?"

Merle intervened.

"Both of you shut the hell up. It's alright. Someone needs to keep watch anyhow." He reached for his door handle. "Now let's get to it."

"Reckon I'll sit with her," Randy said.

Freah looked at Randy strangely. Was this a trap? Is he planning to send killers inside the house after them? Or was she allowing her paranoia to get the best of her?

Freah looked at Colleen. Could she trust her best friend these days? Was Colleen jealous of her? Did she want her way of life? Randy was a horrible businessman who was constantly pouring endless drug revenue into half-cocked endeavors, and if it wasn't for Merle's lovable generosity, they would've been up to their necks in debt.

Randy wants to be the next king. Does Colleen second the motion?

Freah hated such thoughts about her best friend, but she didn't know what to believe anymore. Her family was being eradicated by a faceless threat that had proven he means business. How many allies does this fucker have, and how many of them are right here amongst them throughout this trade of bloodshed?

Merle, Freah, Squirrel, and Davie all walked down the street to T-Bass's house as if they were just some friendly visitors, and Randy watched them from the comfort of the driver's seat.

Freah looked over her shoulder at the truck with questionable eyes. What was all that talk about how she doesn't look good in stripes? Why would Colleen fear the possibility of cops unless she felt—or knew—they had a good chance of showing up?

She helped plot and dispose of Franky's body, for heaven's sake.

But nevertheless, something was not right about all of this.

"Sweetie, I need to talk to you," Freah said to Merle. She was no longer able to hold it all in.

Merle looked at her just as he set foot on T-Bass's property.

"Can it wait?" he asked her.

Squirrel brandished a .357 long nose, and Davie slipped some brass knuckles onto his fingers.

Seeing this made Freah retract her intention—now was obviously not the time.

Freah looked back to the truck and saw the blush orange glow of a phone screen.

Who the hell was Randy talking to?

Chapter 18

Merle did just as he said he was going to do and simply walked through the front door of T-Bass's house as if he owned the place. The living room was nicely arranged with blue cotton cashmere furniture, a stone chimney, black tables, rope lamps, and a lemon motif carpet. T-Bass was doing well for himself.

Merle looked at a tear-shaped window that stopped an inch short of touching the ceiling. A black cloud was easing into view of the full moon—obstructing the course of brilliance, which seemed to be the story of his life. There was always a dark cloud, and at this exact instance, his name was Teddy Lee Richardson.

Merle glanced up the staircase, debating whether or not to send Squirrel and Davie to the second floor, but the sound of a blender gave him direction.

They entered the kitchen, which was actually quite sizable, and saw an average-height man who was standing at the stove in a pair of whitey tighties and dress socks. The smell of mixed herbs and bacon indicated what he was cooking. A jailhouse tattoo or a revolver filled the space of his lower back, and a scorpion was on the left region of his shoulder blade. He had a prosthetic leg with deep scarring of the thighs. This was definitely their guy.

Merle looked at Davie and nodded. Merle had given his brothers strict orders not to cause any bodily harm to T-Bass—he had something else in store for the bastard. Davie moved swiftly across the black linoleum floor, and just as T-Bass turned from the stove with an empty bacon package in his hand, Davie grabbed him in a bear hug, picked him up into the air, and squeezed him in the likeness of a vice. T-Bass yelled and struggled to free himself, but his feeble attempt was to no avail, and within the following minutes, he had tuckered himself out.

Reaching into his pocket for a silk headscarf of Freah's, Merle gave it to Squirrel and told him, "Tie 'em up and sit 'em in a chair." The soft fabric wouldn't chafe the skin and leave markings around his wrists. "And turn that darn blender off."

Merle retrieved the medical pouch from Freah, then took a seat at the table. Freah joined him. Merle unzipped the sack, and Freah saw a syringe, two bottles of insulin labeled *Lantus, Fast Acting*, a glucose meter, and some alcohol pads. She cocked a brow. Diabetic medicine? How is this relevant, right now?

Merle drew a huge dosage of insulin into the needle, then stood up from his chair. T-Bass was keeled over, breathing laboriously. Merle pushed the tip of the syringe into the fatty tissue of T-Bass's upper arm, then reclaimed his seat next to Freah.

T-Bass looked up at his aggressors and immediately recognized Merle. He was a ratty-looking man with thick, oily brown hair and sharp cheekbones.

"Dirty Merle," T-Bass said with a sneer.

Squirrel and Davie looked to one another questionably. *Dirty Merle?*

"Don't call me that," Merle said with heat to his tone that sizzled.

T-Bass scoffed. It was obvious this man held some resentment toward Merle. "What else is there to call a slimy, backstabbing sumbitch like yourself?"

Again, Squirrel and Davie shared a look. Freah was equally confused because Merle hadn't told them that him and T-Bass had a past.

T-Bass snapped. "Look at me." Spittle flew from his lip. "You did this!"

Merle snapped. "You did it to yourself. Now where's my damn son?"

T-Bass grinned. "I know nothing of your son. I'm a pastor, for crying out loud. I'm for the Lord, boy."

Merle knew a lie when he heard one, and he wasted no time calling him out on it. "You're not fooling nobody with this church shit, boy. You're crooked as a hook and taking these town folks for a ride. Now I know you're still in cahoots with Teddy Lee, so if you care to live any longer, you best get to talking, hear?"

T-Bass spit across the table onto Merle's hand and sleeve. "Go to hell, you rotten scaliwag."

Squirrel went for his pistol, but Merle raised his hand to stop him, saying, "Tend to them fiddlers before they burn, little brother."

Squirrel did as he was told, but not before spitting in T-Bass's face and telling him, "Try that shit again and I'll kill ya' dead, punk."

Merle wiped his hand on the thigh of his jeans. "He's overprotective. So I'd watch it, if I were you," he said to T-Bass.

"Do with me as you will. I'm—"

Freah cut him off. "Where is our fucking son, you bastard?"

T-Bass looked at her curiously. "So this the old lady, huh, Merle? The bitch you cheated on with Bobbi Dupree?"

"You don't know what you're talking about, boy, and you never thought to ask, either," Merle said. "Just couldn't help but be Teddy Lee's fucking lapdog. Now you're a fucking cripple, because—"

T-Bass shouted angrily. "Because of you, you motherfucker, and I'll never forget it." . . .

Way Back When

. . . T-Bass sped around the bend of Stonecreek Road in his brand-new 2006 Pontiac Firebird. His good pal, Teddy Lee, was in the passenger seat, and they were rocking out to some pretty sick tunes. Tonight was special. Teddy Lee had purchased the biggest diamond ring that T-Bass had ever laid eyes on, and they were on their way to his gal's house so he could take a knee. Bobbi Dupree was a fine specimen and had successfully stolen Teddy Lee's heart from all the other gals in Lee County.

The town was in full bloom. The mines issued payroll checks today, so the economy was booming. Folks were out and about in their finest duds in search of a good time, and by George, was it out there to be found. Ballrooms, brothels, and bars thrived; matinees and public outings to the yearly carnival and beer fest on the outskirts drew crowds from far and near—Lee County was the place to be.

"Now, Imma need ya' to hurry this here thang on up, Teddy," T-Bass said while taking a moment to look in his rearview mirror to smooth out his eyebrows. "'Cause I got a date with Tina Dawson."

Teddy Lee smiled. "You can't rush love, my friend." His smile grew taller. "And Imma spend the rest of my life with this gal." Teddy Lee punched him playfully on the arm. "So sit tight and tell Tina I'm sorry."

The two pals spoke further about life and love, but it wasn't until T-Bass turned onto Bobbi Dupree's street that Teddy Lee began to get cold feet.

"Am I doing the right thing?" Teddy Lee asked T-Bass. He was nervous. "I mean, this is a big step, you know? Lotta respon—"

T-Bass cut in. "You're gonna be everything she needs you to be, friend. She's gonna be just as nervous as . . ."

Turning into the driveway of Bobbi Dupree's house, T-Bass tapped his brake so as not to hit a man who was down on his knees, spewing his fucking guts out.

"Is that . . . is that Randy?" Teddy Lee said.

"Look like 'em. Ain't that Merle's car?"

Opening his door, Teddy Lee said, "What the hell are they doing here?"

Teddy Lee looked at Randy, then ran to the front door just as it swung open and he found himself standing toe-to-toe with Merle, who was his friend and coworker at Steckenburg Mines.

Teddy Lee looked at Bobbi. She was standing to Merle's right—barely dressed in nothing, looking as guilty as sin.

Teddy Lee punched Merle in his face and felt bone crunch beneath the pressure of his knuckles.

***

. . . "Alright. That's enough," Merle said, interrupting T-Bass's reflection on that night in Lee County.

T-Bass looked Freah square in the eyes and said, "We treated this numbskull like family, and what does he do? Screws Bobbi Dupree behind his pal's back and gets her pregnant, by God." He cut his eyes to Merle. "Explain the child, asshole. Tell her the truth."

Merle looked at Freah. T-Bass's words cut deep, and she appeared as though she wanted to cry.

"I swear to you. I never—"

Freah cut Merle off. "The child this bastard speaks of doesn't matter. We're here to find our son." She emphasized the word *'our.'*

T-Bass's shit-eating grin faded. He had always heard that she worshiped Merle, but to see it firsthand made him think about his Tina—damn, he screwed that relationship up.

Freah averted her glare to T-Bass. "So if you think for one minute that your little story is gonna throw us off your scent, you're about as stupid as you look, 'cause I'll chop ya' pecker off and feed it to you, buddy."

Squirrel and Davie both slapped their knees. They loved the fire that surged throughout their sister-in-law's veins.

"Teddy Lee will have that damn formula of y'all's and y'all's fucking heads," T-Bass said with a grit, then released a short laugh.

"Where is he?" Merle asked.

"The devil's everywhere."

"No. I'm right here."

Merle lit a cigarette, and Freah followed suit. In due time, T-Bass would be changing his tune.

Davie raided the fridge and helped himself to the bacon on the stove.

Squirrel swiped a newspaper off the counter and said, "Imma go feed the fish . . . (take a shit) . . . Yell if ya' need me."

T-Bass sat silently with his thoughts. Even now, at this time when he no longer rode with the Infidels, his loyalty remained whole.

Thirty minutes passed, and T-Bass had begun to perspire. "What did you do to me?" he asked, feeling weak. "What'd you give me?" He was panicking.

Insulin is a good way of killing people because it leaves no trace of toxin in the stomach or elsewhere, and disappears very quickly once in the bloodstream. Death by shock.

"You're dying," Merle told him. "Your glucose level has dropped to the point of putting you in shock."

T-Bass puked all over himself.

"If you don't eat or drink something soon, you're gonna die, boy."

Squirrel raised a glass of orange juice and said, "Where is he?"

The abnormal decrease of sugar in his blood spiked, and T-Bass felt like complete and utter shit—he needed that glass of orange juice.

"Chicken Hawk," T-Bass said. "I'm meeting him at . . ." He swallowed. "At Chicken Hawk's house tomorrow."

Merle looked at his brothers. Chicken Hawk worked for them and ran their meth operation in Inkly Bottom, the black area of Norton. Squirrel was the one who brought Chicken Hawk into the fold as a man who could uphold their product in that section.

Hearing this pissed them all off, because not only had Chicken Hawk betrayed them, but he also had the audacity to attend Dog Man's funeral.

"Why are you meeting him at Chicken Hawk's house? Does he have our son there?" Freah asked him.

"I don't know. But it's where we all meet him to score our product."

"You're selling drugs out of the church?" Davie said with disbelief. "Unbelievable."

They questioned T-Bass until that white light reached out and grabbed him. Then, Davie and Squirrel carried his body into the living room and sat it in the recliner with the remote control in his hand.

It was time to end this. They left the way they came in—quietly.

Chapter 19

The couple was dressed and back to the basics of preparing their hoorah, but the lingering relaxation of good sex was still present throughout their bodies.

Harley diced a carrot, then raked the small cubes into a pot of boiling broth. She was having the best of times, and so was he. She looked over at him as he grilled two monstrous-sized cheeseburgers. He must've felt her eyes on him because he looked at her with that dazzling white smile of his.

"What?" he asked her. "Why you looking at me like that?"

"I have something I wanna give you."

"You too? 'Cause so do I."

She beamed. "Oh, really?" She placed her palm out. "You first, then."

He reached for a spoonful of cream cheese and plopped it in her hand. Harley suppressed her smile and placed one hand on her hip.

"Real funny, bozo."

"Oh, you were expecting something else?" he teased.

"You darn tootin' I am," she wiped her hand onto a towel. "Now gimme, asshole."

Errol raised a brow. "Give you some asshole?" he said, looking horrified but hardly capable of containing his humor. "I love you, but it ain't that kind of gathering, sugar."

Harley's smile slowly melted away, and she wondered if he realized what he just said to her.

Errol saw the look on her face and immediately felt like he kicked himself in the ass. Revealing his inner feelings this early in the rodeo would surely run her away.

"Reckon I'll go first," Errol said, quick to change the subject but eager to give her his present. "When I carved our initials in that tree, I was gonna cut a heart around it, but figured there was no place to put it."

He reached inside his pants pocket and came out with something small enough to conceal in his fist.

"What is it?" Harley asked him.

Errol opened his hand, revealing an empty palm, but said, "My heart."

She laughed. "Well, for one, why would your heart be inside your pocket, and why is it so tiny? Invisible, really." Her laughter made him smile.

"Well, if you must know. The—"

"Yes, I must know, sir," she teased.

"The last gal I was with broke my heart. So, to keep that from happening again, I put it up for safe keeping."

Her smile vanished. Safe keeping? Was he trusting her with his heart?

"Take it," he told her, smiling.

She took the imaginative heart from his hand. "And where would I put it?"

"Reckon where it belongs. With yours."

Harley felt her va-jay-jay twitch and her heart flutter with excitement. She reached into her back pocket for a folded sheet of notebook paper and gave it to him.

"What's this?" Errol asked her.

"My thoughts. Whenever I'm not with you, I think about you so much. So I started writing it out. That way, I can give you my all—no gaps between your and my feelings, no absent moments in our relationship."

This touched Errol; a double tap.

"Wow," was all he could say.

"I'd like for us to do things like this," Harley shared. "Can we, baby?" Her eyes and tone were as soft as cotton.

Errol was putty in her hands. He had thought of this moment for quite some time, but so had she.

"We sure can," he answered.

She beamed. "Read it."

Errol opened the letter.

Errol,

As I sit here at home, struggling to focus on my homework, all I can seem to think about is you, your touch, smile, hiss, us, and how the thought of forever makes me happy. Although young, I seem to have a sense of what's real and what's not, and this, this what you and I share, is real, realer than anything I've ever experienced before. The way you talk with me, and not to me, the way you see me for who I am, instead of who I'm not, or who you want me to be, and I like that a lot. I feel as though this is all a dream, that the likes of you can't be true, but thoughts of your soft kisses and big hands all over me reminds me that yes, Harley, Errol is really yours ... forever. And I will never let you down.

Love, Harley

Errol looked up from the letter and Harley kissed him.

Chapter 20

Rock-on was sitting bedside, his thoughts off someplace else, as the *beep-beep*, *shling-shling*, *bip-bip* of multiple machines sang throughout the background of his contemplative state. The oxygen pump went, *sloomp-sloomp*, and then there was the interference of the Yankees vs Mets game on the flat-screen television.

Sitting before him was a cold plate of food: two slices of pepperoni pizza, French fries, and a condensed Dixie cup of cola. He couldn't eat a thing. The mere smell of the ketchup made him nauseous.

Rock-on held on to Savannah's hand. The texture of her palm was smooth and soft, but the bloody bandage that was wrapped around her wrist tainted the richness of the touch.

His brothers were right—he needed to stay put. Savannah needed him here and not off somewhere chasing a goddamn ghost. But damn if he didn't have the urge to hurt someone, really, really bad. However, it was like Merle used to always tell him when they were boys. "You ain't gone bust a grape in a fruit fight, boy. So you best be who you are before you really get yourself hurt."

Rock-on had never been the violent sort, and he had run from more fights than a little bit, or allowed his brothers to fight his battles for him, which they were more than happy to oblige. He just wasn't anything like his brothers, and he remembered the disappointing look in his pa's eyes whenever he would show a less manly approach to anything his father deemed 'Man Shit.' But eventually, Rock-on had come to accept that he was a lover and not a fighter. What is so bad about that?

Rock-on thought about his daughters and the future humiliation that they could possibly experience once town folk shared his background of a worthless hound dog who lacked respect for their mother or women in general. Was that the legacy that he wanted? An out-of-control adulterer who didn't lift a damn finger to avenge the fatal attempt on his wife's life? What kind of person would proudly want someone like that for their parents? He had let Savannah and their children down.

These disturbing revelations caused him to rise up from his chair and pace the floor. Stopping to gaze out the window into the night, his eyes settled on the outer traffic of Madison Avenue. He considered a few things: Moving away from Norton and never returning. Quitting the drug trade and opening his very own auto repair shop. He had always been good at fixing vehicles. Renewing his vows to Savannah and this time honoring and upholding his words. Dedicating himself to fatherhood and raising his girls to the best of his ability.

Rock-on wondered what his brothers were up to. Did they find Errol? Who the hell has Squirrel killed?

He looked over his shoulder at Savannah. Her face was wrapped like one of them Egyptian mummies that he'd seen in the movies—she was in a coma. It just didn't seem worth it, and a part of him wanted to somehow reach out to Teddy Lee and give him Dog Man's concoction. Rock-on was beginning to believe that it was the only way to end this madness. Too many lives had been lost over some damn drugs. Was there not enough money to go around?

Dog Man and Merle started selling meth to provide for the family once pa died, but somewhere along the lines, they all lost sight of their cause. They had accumulated more than enough money and property, so why not just let Teddy Lee and his boys have it? Rarely does anyone make it for as long as they have in the area. So, maybe this is a sign that it's time for them to take a bow and close the curtain while they still have something to hold on to.

A tear rolled down his cheek, wetting some prickles of his five o'clock shadow. Dog Man. Jaxon. Savannah. This was not some random bar-room beef between them and a group of ignorant cowhands. These bikers were cold-blooded killers, and they weren't going anywhere no time soon.

"I can stop this," he said quietly.

But there was only one problem. Only Dog Man and Merle knew the ingredients that boosted the quality of their ice, but Dog Man was a hoarder, so somewhere in his house was that chemical recipe that would back the Infidels off from the family. Lisette and the kids were in Kingsport at Merle's warehouse, so the time to search their house was now.

Grabbing his coat from off the back of the chair, Rock-on kissed Savannah on her lips, then hurried out the door where he ran into a good friend of his.

"Whoa," said the friend. "Where you off to, bro?"

Rock-on was surprised to see him. "You came."

"Of course, you kidding? How is she?"

His expression saddened. "Not good."

The two men spoke further, carrying the conversation to the elevator doors. Rock-on really appreciated the concern and support for Savannah; his friend's sincerity was genuine, and it touched his heart.

Some nurses came running past, and Rock-on watched them, hoping that they weren't headed to Savannah's room—they bypassed her door, and he released a breath of relief. The elevator doors parted with a 'Ding,' and the two men docked the platform.

Reaching the bottom floor, Rock-on and his pal hurried across the floor of the waiting room, unaware of the two men who stood up from their seats to follow him.

Chapter 21

The bunch were gathered in a C.V.S. parking lot, and the raucous of the neighboring lumber yard caused them to speak louder than usual.

"It just doesn't make much sense, is all," Squirrel said, standing amongst the headlights of his Hellcat. "Why the sam hell would he help a band of dickheads take us out?"

Davie, blowing into the palms of his hands to ward off the chill, said, "Chicken Hawk has always been a greedy little bastard."

"Reckon none of that matters right now, do it?" Merle said, twisting the lid off a beer. "Teddy Lee's using anyone who's quick to change coats on us. Probably tend to kill 'em no sooner than later."

Everyone nodded agreeably.

"Turn Chicken Hawk into chicken gizzards," Randy said.

"Serves 'em right," said Squirrel. "That dirty fuck is still holding a kilo and a half of our dope, too."

Merle looked over his shoulder at Freah, who was talking on her phone in search of information about Errol and Harley. A great cousin of Merle's, who was a roofing contractor, so happened to do a job for Bobbi Dupree several months ago and still had her address on file. But upon returning to Norton tonight, they drove directly to Bobbi's house—no one was home and her phone number had been changed. Another dead end.

"Where we gonna put 'em only calls for a suit," Davie said. "And a goddamn pray, by George."

"Tomorrow," Randy said, turning to get inside his truck where Colleen awaited.

"Six-thirty," Merle said, speaking of the time that Teddy Lee was supposed to arrive at Chicken Hawk's house.

Randy waved his hand. "I'll be there," he said over his shoulder.

Merle nodded to his brothers, then headed for his truck as well, telling Freah, "Let's go, darling."

"To hell with getting that sumbitch tomorrow," Squirrel said to Davie. "We're gone take his ass out tonight."

Davie quickly looked toward Merle's direction, silently hoping that he didn't overhear Squirrel. "He ain't gone take too brightly to that."

"Dark as this situation has gotten, I reckon there's no room for light. Come on."

They got into the Hellcat, and Squirrel peeled rubber, fishtailing out the lot.

"He gone wrap a pole in that damn car one day," Merle said, shaking his head.

Freah sighed sadly. "Where is our baby, Merle?"

"I don't know, sweety. But—"

In a teary tone of voice, she snapped, "But nothing. You do something, dammit. You fix this." She broke down. "They're holding him somewhere, I know it. He don't even have his medication, Merle."

Unbeknownst to anyone outside of Freah and Merle, Errol had sickle cell anemia and had a regiment of medication and health shakes to follow. Errol was a proud kid, and he strongly felt as though people would treat him differently if his condition was ever revealed, so Freah and Merle respected his wish to keep it amongst themselves.

Merle didn't feel as though Freah was openly attacking him. She was hurting but aware that he was possibly the only person who could bring their son to safety—if he was still breathing, that is. But they refused to believe that Errol was dead.

Merle pulled out of the lot and headed north in the direction of the house. It had been a long day, but he doubted that sleep would come easily.

They rode in silence, and silence was the enemy because it allowed their thoughts to talk, to talk too loudly without any distraction. So, the notion of drowning his misery in a bottle of whiskey was highly enticing, so appealing that Merle agreed to the terms and opened the console for his bottle of rye. He tipped the rim to his lips for a strong gulp. The faster he got drunk, the better. His guilty conscience was a relentless heifer that wouldn't stop nagging at him for bringing this murderous bastard to their doorstep. Real men are protectors, but right now, he felt more like a saboteur whose choices in life would ultimately uproot his family tree if he didn't kill Teddy Lee.

Freah reached for the bottle, saying to him, "It's time you tell me."

Merle looked at her. He knew this was coming.

"Everything," she said, then took a swig of whiskey that caused her to make a face as the burning sensation whisked down her esophagus. "What happened with you and Teddy Lee? And why the hell you suddenly looked constipated when you saw that gal, Harley?" She sniffed. "Just give it to me from the shoulders. I'm a big gal, I can handle the truth."

Merle lit a cigarette. "I've never laid a hand on Bobbi Dupree. She—"

Freah interrupted him, saying, "Then who did?"

Merle exhaled a plume of smoke. He promised to never speak of that night again.

Freah opened her phone and enlarged the photograph of Holly. Showing Merle the image of the girl, she said, "'Cause this gal looks a lot like fucking Randy."

Merle shook his head. He had always known about Harley and Holly and the abnormal pregnancy that divided the two, but it had nothing to do with him at all, although Teddy Lee had forever thought otherwise.

"Obviously your loyalty to your pal is why you're not—"

Merle cut in. "No. My loyalty to you is why I ain't spoken about it."

This baffled Freah, and the look on her face told as much.

Merle continued. "You wanna know what happened, Freah?" . . .

. . . Merle was sitting in a chair outside Randy's motel room. The night was warm, and children were frolicking in the swimming pool below as adults conversed amongst the smoke of short-legged grills and ice coolers. Someone had seasoned their hamburgers perfectly, reminding Merle that he hadn't eaten since lunch today.

Merle took a swig of beer, then looked up at the sky. Space had always intrigued him, but the stars especially. What was it that made them burn so brightly, for so long?

The phone rang, and Merle got up from his chair to enter the room.

"Hello," he answered the call.

"Hey, hon," came Freah's voice. "What you doing?"

"Just sitting out, having a beer, baby. Reckon I'll see you bright and early."

Merle had a big fat check in his wallet from Steckenburg Mining Company, and the day after every paycheck, Randy and him drove home to Norton to give their hard-earned money to their wives. They had families to take care of and were normally left with nothing afterwards, but men don't cry over spilled milk—they just simply wipe it up and move on.

"Well, I'll be waiting with bells on. I miss you," Freah told him.

"I miss y'all too. Reckon Errol's asleep?"

"Yeah. So is your pa'."

"How's he doing?"

"He didn't do so well today. He's . . ." Her words trailed off.

Merle's father had fallen ill to Parkinson's disease, which was what prompted him to get a job in the coal mines of Lee County, because he had to keep up with his pa's medical expenses, as well as the household.

"He's not doing too good, hon," Freah finally said. "But Dog Man made him some grits and gravy that made 'em happy."

A small grin crept onto Merle's face. His pa loved grits and gravy more than anything.

"Good," he said softly.

"Merle, where's my other half?" came Colleen's high-pitched voice from the background.

"Colleen wanna talk to Randy, hon."

Merle glanced toward the door, thinking of a plausible lie to tell Colleen. Randy was a full-fledged horn dog who had driven his marriage to the very edge.

"One more hussy, Randy. Just one more, and I'm walking out that front door, I swear for God, I will," Colleen had told Randy just a few months ago.

"Uh, he went to grab us a bite to eat," Merle lied. Randy was really off somewhere with some random brocade who Merle had never met before. "But I'll tell 'em to give her a call."

Freah and Merle spoke for several more minutes, then ended the call with their ritual: "I love you." "I love you more." "That's impossible." "That's what I was thinking."

Just when Merle walked out the door, the phone rang. Figuring that it was Freah calling back, Merle backtracked to the bedside table.

"Yello," he answered.

"Merle," said a panicked voice.

Merle didn't recognize the tone. "Who is this?"

"Bobbi. I need for you to come to my house right now and get Randy," she was fast-talking to him. "He's drunk and refusing to leave, and Teddy Lee just called. He's on his fucking way over here, and—"

Merle couldn't believe his ears. Why the hell would Randy and Bobbi do something like this? Teddy Lee was a good guy, and he had been nothing but friendly and helpful to them since they came to Lee County for work.

"You're shitting me, right?" Merle said angrily.

"Merle, please. Teddy Lee will kill—"

"Okay, okay, okay. I'm on my way." . . .

. . . Freah interrupted Merle, saying softly, "I remember that night. Colleen said you were lying, that she could feel it."

"Well, she felt right. Sumbitch was dog drunk and naked as a blue jay when I got there. Hell-bent about Bobbi answering Teddy Lee's call while they were bumping uglies, ya' know? Stupid as all outdoors, these two."

"But T-Bass said that when they got there, Randy was—"

"Outside throwing a rod. After me and Bobbi dressed the fool and got 'em in the car, the son of a gun got to crying about his goddamn wallet."

"He left it in the house?" she assumed.

Merle released a heavy breath. "Yep, and without that paycheck of his, Colleen—"

"Would've lost it."

"So I ran back in to get it, and next thing I know, Teddy Lee's at the damn door."

"Y'all fought?"

"Like our lives depended on it. Tore through that house like bulls, I tell ya'. But once he ran inside that closet—"

"Closet?" Freah's eyes stretched. She was really locked in on the details.

"Yeah. I ran like hell." . . .

. . . Teddy Lee grabbed Merle by his throat and slammed the back of his head into a mirror.

"Teddy Lee, stop it!" Bobbi pleaded. "You're gonna kill 'em."

Seven years of bad luck, but Teddy Lee didn't give a flying fuck about that mirror—his heart bled murder.

Merle headbutted Teddy Lee, then slung him onto the bed. Teddy Lee kicked Merle in the stomach, causing him to double over in pain. Teddy Lee kicked that bastard again, this time in his fucking face.

Bobbi yelped. She was a frantic mess.

Merle flailed backwards and landed on his ass. Teddy Lee dove on top of him—the back of Merle's head smacked into a dresser drawer, and the brass handle split his flesh wide.

"Ugh," Merle grunted painfully.

Teddy Lee punched him in the face and shouted, "Backstabbing sum—"

Merle grabbed a piece of the mirror and drove the sharp edge into Teddy Lee's arm.

"No!" Bobbi cried. "Stop it, you two!"

Merle socked Teddy Lee in the jaw, then shoved him aside. Teddy Lee rolled toward the wall, then scrambled to the closet door on his hands and knees.

"Merle, run!" Bobbi yelled in a tear-stricken voice.

Merle staggered out the bedroom door and fell against the opposite wall. *Doom, doom, doom, doom, doom, doom*—the pulsating throb of his heartbeat in his ears. And just when he stumbled a few feet forward, the monstrous quake of a shotgun rang true, and the wall ate a handful of buckshots.

"No-good bastard!" Teddy Lee hollered. Damn, was he mad.

Merle ran for the door, praying to a god he'd never believed in, promising to believe in him if he delivered him safely from this mess. He thought of Freah. Errol. His brothers. He had so much more that he wanted to say to them—particularly, "I love you."

It can't end like this. He did nothing wrong. Why does he have to die for another man's mistake?

Merle ran out the front door, wild-eyed and out of breath, and saw someone beating the living hell out of Randy. Merle grabbed the man from behind in a yoke and whirled around with him, just as Teddy Lee pulled the trigger . . .

. . . "He shot T-Bass?" Freah said.

Merle nodded. "Sure did."

"Is that how he lost his leg?"

"No. From how I heard it, the wound in his thigh got infected, and he neglected to return to the hospital like a normal fucking gent."

Freah passed him the bottle of whiskey. They were nearly to the house, and they both were silently hoping to see Errol's pickup truck parked in the driveway.

"Luckily, Teddy Lee only had those two shots, and he was so wrapped up with tending to T-Bass that I was able to gather Randy in the car and high-tail it out of there."

Freah nodded, remembering Merle coming home that night. "Bar fight. You said some hardheads started trouble with y'all," she said.

Merle nodded, then took a swig.

"Why didn't you just tell me the truth, Merle?"

"I couldn't. Randy feared losing Colleen if the truth ever came out."

"But it's me. If you would've told me to keep it between us, I—"

"He knew about Franky, Freah."

This took her off guard.

"Colleen told him about us killing your brother, and in so many words, he basically told me that he'd keep our secret if I kept his, and even more so when we heard that Bobbi was pregnant."

Freah was disgusted by this. “And you consider this a friend?” she said.

“Reckon no more than you should consider Colleen one.”

He had her there. How many more people had Colleen told about that night?

“Just best to keep your enemies close,” Merle said with a shrug. “That way you’ll know exactly how to kill ‘em,” he met her gaze. “And where.” He pointed, and Freah followed his finger, which led her eyes toward her window.

Freah’s mouth fell open, and she cocked her head to one side. As they rode past the parking lot of a Piggly Wiggly grocery store, she couldn’t believe her eyes.

Chapter 22

Squirrel pulled into a vacant lot of an old radio station and parked. Across the street was Walnut Terrace—a five-story apartment building that was completely overrun by crime and drugs. Inkly Bottom was considered the "quote on quote" hood of Norton, and although not very big, the area was big on trouble. To the right of Walnut Terrace was a run-down laundromat and corner store, and to its left was a residential neighborhood of low-income houses that has seen better days. A few stragglers loitered about, but for the most part, things appeared quiet.

"You sure he's here?" Davie asked. He didn't care much for this side of town.

"He wasn't home. This the only other place I've ever met him at."

"Reckon he got our dope in there with 'em?"

Squirrel looked at him with a wolfish grin, and said, "And more." He cocked his gun. "Let's go."

They got out of the car and jogged across the street. The wind carried litter down the road and a pissy odor escaped an alley between the laundromat and corner store that smacked them in their faces unexpectedly. This was a place of broken dreams and empty promises.

Entering the building, their eyes adjusted to the dim lighting and shadowy figures that lurked the hallway: dope fiends. Hip hop blared inside one of the apartments, and the stench of reefer was permanently installed in the walls like the mailboxes.

The elevator was out of order, so Squirrel and Davie had to take the stairs to the fifth floor. Squirrel didn't take kindly to folks who went out of their way to make a fool out of him, so Chicken Hawk was scheduled for a rude awakening.

***

Yashica's little sexy ass crawled onto the queen-size bed, that soft pretty brown ass of hers tooted in the air—pussy calling the name of every man in the bedroom. The orgy was well underway, and pleasurable sounds swelled with the "*Clap, Clap, Clap*" of stone-hard dicks pounding juicy, wet pussies.

Yashica mounted Chicken Hawk's body and slipped his large cock inside her lotus flower. Then Lamar positioned himself behind her and filled her asshole with eight inches of rawness. She bit down on her lip and braced herself for the pressure of two rods. Lamar and Chicken Hawk sealed her in the sandwich and crushed her soul with long and powerful thrusts.

Alongside the trio, Gail sucked, licked, and tongued Janeen's pussy while Tony rearranged her guts from behind.

"Shit," she said through slurps of sucking Janeen's clitoris.

Kim received a good facial. Five dicks threw up in her face—the men grunted pleasingly while jacking their loads, smacking the heads of their cocks against her lips and face.

Music from the living room seeped into the bedroom from underneath the door, a door that Brock had Penny's back pent against as he held her in his arms, hammering her pussy in place.

***

Meanwhile In The Living Room . . .

Cornell and Vernon were sitting on the sofa, bagging grams of crack cocaine and meth when a knock came to the door. Reaching for the burning blunt in an ashtray, Cornell took a pull of the chronic weed, then passed the "L" to Vernon.

Coughing, Cornell said in a strained tone of voice, "Oh yeah, that's definitely him." Expressing the potency of the cannabis.

A second knock sounded. Cornell got up to answer the door, feeling no need to grab one of the two guns that were lying on the coffee table.

"Wassup, Candy?" He said upon swinging the door open.

Flashing her snaggle-tooth smile, Candy entered the apartment with a handful of crumpled bills.

"What you got, aunty?" Cornell asked her while pulling his dreadlocks into a ponytail.

"Lemme get a fifty."

Candy gave him the money, and he began to count it, making certain that none of it was counterfeit and the exact amount was on the head. Crack heads were full of cons, and the last time that he was had, Chicken Hawk pistol-whipped him and deducted a week's pay. So he was now thoroughly careful.

Vernon looked around the living room, wondering where the hell did he place that box of sandwich bags.

"Nell, where the rest of the bags at?" he asked Cornell.

"We used 'em. It's some more in the kitchen."

Cornell served Candy a fifty rock, then opened the door for her to leave. Vernon searched a few drawers, moved some things around on top of the refrigerator, and peeked inside a couple of cupboards.

"I don't see 'em," Vernon said.

"Look in the lower cabinets. I think I might've put 'em down there somewhere," Cornell told him just before a knock came to the door.

Cornell opened the door.

***

As soon as the door opened, Davie punched the living daylights out of Cornell, who staggered and fell against the coffee table. Whereupon, simply blinking, Squirrel blew his brains out.

Davie quickly closed the door and turned the music off. Squirrel looked around, and just as he was taking a foot toward the kitchen, noises came from the back of the apartment.

***

Throwing her hips to get the full effect of both dicks, Yashica released a throaty moan. Her juices trickled down their sacks, glistening on their hairs with the mixture of creamy, white cum.

"Fucking bitch, take it, take it," Tony said, ramming his arm inside of Gail's phat pussy as she still feasted on Janeen's goods, slopping her down hungrily.

"A'ight." Brock grunted, nutting in between Penny's butt cheeks—her thick ass loved that sticky sex.

"Daddy. Daddy," Kim whined. "Fuck me, Daddy."

Then the door came crashing down.

***

At full speed, Davie rammed his shoulder into the bedroom door and knocked it off its hinges, startling the occupants.

Davie swung those huge fists of his, knocking Tony and Brock out immediately before kicking Gail off the bed and into the wall.

Janeen released a shrill cry. Chicken Hawk lurched upward to push Yashica and Lamar's weight off of him so he could scramble for his gun that was inside the bedside table drawer, but Squirrel shot both Yashica and Lamar in their heads, pinning him down under their bulk.

“Mothafucka!” Chicken Hawk cursed.

Squirrel leapt up onto the bed, onto his knees, and bit the point of Chicken Hawk’s nose off. Davie looked away, but he will never forget the painful wail that escaped Chicken Hawk’s throat.

Squirrel spit it back into Chicken Hawk’s face and shouted, “Fucking traitor. Talk 'fore I kill ya’. Where’s my goddamn nephew?” He tore into his nose again.

***

Vernon carefully peered into the living room from over the counter of the kitchen. Cornell was dead, that was for sure. Vernon looked at the front door, thinking to make a run for it, but then his eyes swept the two guns that were lying on the coffee table, and he reconsidered. He had the drop on these two fools, plus he would never live it down if he let them get away with killing his homeboy, Cornell.

Vernon ran out from hiding and collected the two weapons. Easing down the hallway, one foot over the other, Vernon took slow, calculated breaths. Could killing a man be this easy?

“Ahhh. Pennington Gap, man. That’s all I know,” he heard Chicken Hawk say. “I swear, that’s all I know, Squirrel, that’s all I know.”

Vernon paused in his tracks upon hearing that it was Squirrel who was in the bedroom. Vernon didn’t know Squirrel, but he knew of him and heard that he was not to be tangled with.

But he killed Cornell.

Hell naw.

Vernon proceeded down the hallway. The smell of raunchy sex was strong.

“I don’t have anything to do with this. Please let me go,” came a woman’s voice. Sounded like Janeen. “I won’t say nothing.”

With both guns extended in his hands, Vernon entered the bedroom, and all hell broke loose.

Chapter 23

Harley opened her mouth to accept a spoonful of macaroni and cheese with pineapples from Errol, and to her surprise, it was fucking awesome.

Harley closed her eyes and savored the flavors.

"Umm. Now that is really fucking good," she admitted.

Errol took a bite, and his features lit up.

"Damn," he said. "Our experiments were actually pretty damn good."

Harley smiled.

"This will sell."

Errol slapped her a high five.

"Let's discuss packaging."

They laughed.

Seated on the table before them was a small feast for two: fried seafood spaghetti, meatloaf burgers, chicken fried rice with watermelon hot sauce, green beans and eggs with Dijon, deep-fried PB&J sandwiches, honey cakes, avocado balls, salmon croquettes, diced bacon and cabbage, buttery biscuits, and much more.

Of course, they knew they could never eat it all in one sitting, so they agreed to package the leftovers and drive out toward Exit 7 to a secluded area called "Tent City," where the majority of the homeless people resided when they weren't in Midtown panhandling or doing odd jobs.

The barroom was dimly lit, and music played lowly from the sound system. They'd made love twice tonight, danced their souls out, and eaten their little hearts to content. Errol's plans for a perfect night had unfolded without a hitch, and they were having a spectacular time together.

Harley fed Errol a bite of liver and onions. She really enjoyed cooking with him. Errol was so carefree and easygoing . . . so addictively handsome and humorous . . . he had her fiendishly yearning for his love and touch.

While chewing, Errol said with a grin, "Hell fire. That's damn good, honey."

Harley beamed, happy that he liked her cooking.

"Thanks."

"Our children gonna eat good."

Harley's smile evaporated.

Errol saw the change in her disposition and quickly apologized for whatever he supposedly did to make her uncomfortable.

"No, it's fine. I'm—"

"No need to explain," he said.

Harley placed her hand gently on top of his.

"Errol, please. It's not like that. I love children."

"Uh-huh," he said, reaching for his beer. He didn't want to ruin the moment, but it was obvious that the mere mention of children negatively affected her mood.

Harley wanted to kick herself in the ass because Errol was very family-oriented, and the last thing she wanted him to believe was that she disliked children.

"My mom," she began, "my mom wasn't all that great. She's done a lot of bad things, you know." She lowered her eyes. "I had a little brother."

The word "had" leapt out at Errol like a jack-in-the-box.

"He was born autistic. His name was Sterling, and me and Holly just loved him to death," she looked into Errol's eyes. "But my mama hated him. She had gotten pregnant by this cowpoke from Montana. Gent was just passing through, really, and after a few weeks of work on Mr. Clint's ranch, he was gone. Mam never really took breakups well, or rather the thought of rejection, I reckon, and began mistreating Sterling. The more he started to look like that stranger, the madder she got, I tell ya'." Her eyes watered. "Then one day she took it too far . . ."

. . . Bristol was the birthplace of country music, but the town was far more unique than the huge image of a guitar that Harley was staring at as her school bus rode down State Street. There was a digital clock counting the remaining 24 hours before an annual NASCAR race gathered at the track on Volunteer Parkway, so the town was currently overwhelmed with excited race fans who commonly referred to themselves as "Rednecks United."

Harley looked ahead at a large decorative sign of lights that read, "Welcome to Bristol," with two arrows at each end pointing at VA-TN. State Street was actually the state line of Virginia/Tennessee. But Harley couldn't help but feel that it was all just one town—another place that her mother figured she could just up and run to, hiding from her checkered past.

Bristol and Lee County shared similar traits—traditional scenery that was both wholesome and welcoming. The natives walked with an easy strut, as if they'd never been in a rush in their lives, but Harley missed Lee County, her friends, school, and her mamaw's succotash stew and cranberry pudding.

While passing the train station, Harley wished that she could run away to a faraway place and never return, but a nine-year-old could only make it so far before requiring help. Plus, she could never abandon Sterling, so she was stuck with this cruddy way of life until further notice.

Minutes later, the bus neared her apartment building in Rice Terrace—a housing project of significant size but of very few white people.

Harley reached for her backpack that was lying alongside her—a gesture that said, "I don't want anyone sitting here." Then she got to her feet to exit the bus. She could feel their eyes boring holes through her. The new student was always subjected to scrutiny, but Harley didn't care. Let them pick her apart with their beady little eyes—it didn't make them any more black, or her any more white in her opinion.

Stepping out onto Clinton Avenue, Harley glanced at a corner full of men wearing more gold than a little bit. She recognized a few of them. They'd come to the apartment to sell her mother crack cocaine on several occasions. Lee County didn't have many Black families in the area, so Harley didn't know squat about their culture, but she was quickly learning the difference.

The distinctive wail of sirens closed in, drawing her eyes over her shoulder. An ambulance turned onto the street and sped past her, and for some odd reason, a deeply profound sense of worry rocked her. Thoughts of her siblings raced through her mind, but the question was—why?

Harley ran between the gray-colored buildings and rushed out onto West Maple Street, and sure enough, paramedics were hurrying into the door of her apartment. Holly was standing at the foot of the steps in her nightgown—crying.

Harley took off like the wind. "Holly!" she shouted.

"He's dead, Harley. He—he—he." Holly stammered.

Harley shot past her sister, heart drumming dangerously inside her chest, pounding her rib cage, breathing was strenuous, as panic swelled to the proportion of a balloon. She barged into the apartment, and there she stood—her she-devil of a mother, crocodile tears and all.

"What'd you do?" Harley shouted while staring down at Sterling on the floor. A pair of scissors was jammed into the center of his chest, and he wasn't moving. The paramedics were working frantically to revive him.

"I didn't do anything," Bobbi countered. "He—he, I—I told him not to run with them scissors in his hand, and—"

"Liar!"

"Hush, Harley, dammit!" Bobbi stamped her foot. "Go to your room."

"No. You did this."

"Harley, shut up!"

"I'm calling the law."

Bobbi grabbed Harley strongly by her arm, and the paramedics looked at her strangely, a fleeting observation of disapproval . . .

. . . "He died?" Errol said carefully, not wanting to overstep any bounds.

Harley wiped her eyes with a napkin. "Yeah."

"Damn."

"An accidental death, or so they called it, but I knew otherwise. I could feel it, ya' know? She hated him, but it wasn't until she cashed in on the insurance claim that folks around Rice Terrace started talking, and I didn't look like some rebellious brat with mommy issues."

Errol narrowed his eyes. E didn't completely understand. "Insurance? What's so strange—"

"Nothing's strange about having insurance on your children. What is strange is when you don't put insurance on yourself or your two older twins as well."

Errol got it. "Just Sterling."

"Just him," she wiped her nose. "So she did what she was good at. Packed us up and moved us back to Lee County, where she showboated her newfound fortune, basically giving it away in an attempt to buy back her good name, which was never free of mud, nohow."

Silence edged in, nudging the two into their inner thoughts, but they maintained eye contact.

Errol could see that the death of her brother still deeply affected her. "Thank you for sharing that with me," he said. "And I'm sorry for your loss. I know it's hard."

"I have a fear of being her, Errol."

"Your mom?"

"Yeah. What if I somehow inherited her ways, but don't recognize it until it's too late and I have this child on my hands, ya' know?"

"Darling, it's actually the complete opposite. You're gonna go out your way not to be like your momma, instead. Or at least that's how I see it. Sure, bad traits are passed down through generations at times, but most folks don't notice them until they're actually carrying 'em out themselves. You, on the other hand, are carrying the burden of not wanting to carry them out, period. And that's different, sugar. Way different, I tell ya'. You're at a stage of preventing the unknown from happening by not allowing it to happen at all. Show control, which your momma knew nothing about."

Harley smiled, because he really had a way of getting to her. Boys in school didn't talk like Errol.

"And to have control means to have patience, which is one of the most important factors of having children—patience, darling, patience."

Errol poured them a drink. He spoke his peace and didn't see no point in grinding his insight to mush, because her expression revealed the fact that she understood him perfectly fine.

"You're right. She has no patience for motherhood. She has always chosen men over us. Never the one to show any real interest in what we wanted, or wanted to be." She sighed as a flood of bad memories hit her. "Most of the time, I hate to go home, you know?"

Errol nodded. "Makes you wanna have a happy home, doesn't it?"

Harley smiled. His question really resonated, because she used to pray as a girl for God to change her mother's heart and make their household whole and lovingly active, and her Errol was reminding her of her very words for deliverance.

"Yes. I've always wanted that."

"Well, there you have it."

Harley stared into his eyes admiringly. "How is it that you talk the way you do?" she asked him.

"My ma' and pa' had a few sit-downs with me in life. Taught me to be a decent human being, is all. Don't do what they do, but what they say, kinda thang, ya know?"

"I do."

"Plus, they always remind me to be a teenager first," he said, scooping his hand into a strawberry cake and plopping a huge chunk of dessert in Harley's face.

She screamed. "Errol!"

He hopped up from his chair and ran toward the billiard room.

Harley wiped icing from her eyes and shouted. "Imma kick your ass."

"Gotta catch me first."

"Get back here, Errol."

"Lady, I don't know you."

She laughed, then reached inside her pocket and said, "Well, would you look at this?"

Errol stopped running and turned around curiously.

Harley pulled Errol's imaginary heart, which he had given her earlier tonight, out of her pocket and slung it at a wall.

"Oops. I broke your heart, punk," she said with a giggle.

Errol pointed at her. "You're gonna pay for that, lady."

He gave chase. Harley escaped to the kitchen, and as soon as Errol burst through the door, she doused him with a bin of flour.

"Now hop your hind end in that deep fryer!" she told him.

Now they were having some fun. Making memories that'd last a lifetime.

"Fry your chicken shit ass."

Errol wrestled her to the floor and commenced to tickle her.

Oh, how Harley laughed. This boy was breaking through barriers of pain and resentment and casting sunlight upon her heart. She didn't want to let go of this moment.

Chapter 24

Snowflakes fell with the grace of an autumn leaf, but the air was still and quiet as a church mouse. Deputy Nash was directing traffic as Sheriff Dougherty and his son, Patrick, made their way to the side of the road to assess the crime scene. Benton Avenue was short and fairly narrow with a few open establishments that gave it meaning, but for the most part, it was well off from midtown.

The blue Ford Mustang was totaled, but the towering oak tree was in bad shape, as well. The smell of gasoline was strong, and they could hear it trickling from underneath the vehicle, forming a puddle on the asphalt.

Dougherty looked past the Mustang and into the grove. He saw a number of flashlights throughout the darkness—his deputies were in search of possible evidence.

While staring at several sizable bullet holes in the rear end of the car, Patrick said, "Looks like two-two-three rounds. AR style, most likely."

Dougherty nodded agreeably, then looked around. "No shell casings though," he said. "Must've happened back yonder or so." He jerked his thumb over his shoulder, indicating the streets that were around the corner from Benton.

"This car sure does look mighty familiar, pop."

"Yep. Reckon there's only one like it in town," Dougherty said, flashing his light inside the car. There was blood on the front seats and door panel. "I reckon Rock-on is dead or damn close to it."

"I'd say you're right. Who called it in?"

"Some lady who was passing by. Name Dotson," Dougherty answered, then looked across the street at the Burger Shack. "But I see a better witness."

Patrick followed his father's eyes and saw two surveillance cameras mounted on each corner of the Burger Shack's roof, and without another word, they walked across Benton to the eatery.

A minute later, Dougherty and Patrick were following the manager of the Burger Shack through the back of the restaurant. The place smelled of seasoned beef and burnt cooking oil, and the surroundings were chaotic: loud clanking noises from the pots and pan room, and audible sizzle from the grills, and overhead exhaust fan, and frantic staff members.

"I need lettuce!" yelled a woman.

"Craig, check them tots."

"Damn, Jerry, run me over, why don't you."

Dougherty and Patrick both avoided a few bump-ins, then bypassed the freezer and made a left down a short hallway with terrible carpeting and ugly paneled walls that made Dougherty feel as though he had just teleported to a cheesy mobile home. Entering a break room, the manager, who looked to have had one hamburger too many, unlocked a door with a key—revealing an impressive security system with an espresso machine that was within reach of a fabulous wingback chair.

The manager was of great help. He even told them to help themselves to an espresso, which they wasted no time doing.

"Okay. Well, I'll leave you two to it," said the manager.

Dougherty began to scour through the footage of tonight, fast-forwarding past the time-lapse that the manager initially entered in the data.

Patrick pointed to the screen, saying, "Right there."

Dougherty freeze-framed just as the Mustang fishtailed onto Benton with a white dually truck hot on its tail. A dark figure was suspended from the passenger side window with an assault rifle extended in their hands—fire spat from its muzzle.

"It's how they did Savannah," Patrick said. "These are our shooters."

Dougherty resumed the footage. The Mustang never regained control of the road, weaving dangerously before spinning in a complete 360 and colliding into the tree with amazing force. The dually truck pulled to a halt, and two armed men hopped out of the cab and ran to the wreckage.

Dougherty freeze-framed and zoomed in on the men's faces.

"Sweet Mary and Joseph," he said.

"Please tell me that ain't who I think it is?" said Patrick, completely stumped.

Dougherty looked at his son. He, too, was harboring a perplexed expression. "What the sam hell is going on here?" he said, then averted his eyes back to the screen.

The two men retrieved Rock-on's limp body from the Mustang and carried him to their truck. It was Dog Man and his son, Jaxon.

"This doesn't make any sense," Patrick said, his wheels turning inside his head. "If these two yokels are still alive, which they obviously are, who the hell did Merle and them just bury?"

"Right," Dougherty nodded. "And let's not forget the dead body in Abingdon that was supposedly Jaxon."

"After seeing this, I'm skeptical about that whole Abingdon thing entirely. I mean, do we even know if that call or supposed officer was real?"

Dougherty sighed. "Yeah. I reckon we don't know what's real or what's not at this point."

They watched the video for a second time, both wondering what their next move was going to be.

"Reckon the first order of business should be to alert the family of Rock-on's attack," Patrick said.

Dougherty wrinkled a brow questionably. "Was he really attacked, or is he in cahoots with this god-awful—"

"Bull," Patrick interjected.

"Right. Bullshit."

Patrick agreed with his father's theory. "Reckon we should find out," he said.

"A few thangs, actually. Like who the hell is buried in that hole with Dog Man's headstone on it?"

"Want me to call Tim?"

Tim Gooseman owned a small construction firm in midtown, and in order for them to uproot a grave, they needed a front loader.

"Yeah. And call Anna and tell her to contact the Abingdon Sheriff's Department about that second body."

With a tight nod, Patrick reached inside his pocket for his phone.

Dougherty stared at the screen. Hell has come to Norton, and if he didn't hastily douse water onto this fire, Norton was going to burn to the ground.

Dougherty had known Merle and his family since he was a little boy, and not once did he ever think that he would see them at such odds as they were, right now. Why is Dog Man doing this to his family? Should he consider Lisette as a conspirator? How does a husband keep such treachery from his beloved wife? What is the cause of all this? Murder. An essential act that draws the line in the sand.

Dougherty's radio squawked. "All units report to three-twenty-five Sinclair Avenue, apartment five-fifteen. Reports of shots fired and possible victims."

Dougherty looked at Patrick. That was the address for Walnut Terrace in Inkly Bottom. It was about to be a long night.

Chapter 25

With both guns extended in his hands, Vernon shot Davie three times in his back before Squirrel whirled around and . . .

Vernon pulled the trigger.

Squirrel pulled the trigger.

Fire raced from the muzzles, and the two bullets bypassed one another with a heated exchange.

Vernon shifted with a lean.

Squirrel bent his knees and slightly turned.

But neither of the men was swift enough to avoid the slugs. Squirrel caught him in his shoulder, and the tremendous force of the bullet spun him around and dropped him—he hit the bedside table face-first.

The back of Vernon's head exploded on the wall with a sickening splat—he died on his feet, never feeling the impact of the fall.

Chicken Hawk squirmed from underneath the weight of the dead bodies and quickly gathered his clothes from off of the floor. He was currently on probation, so he had to make way before he found himself back in the slammer.

***

Merle pulled into the parking lot of Rent-A-Center and parked in a space that faced the Piggly Wiggly across the street.

"As soon as Colleen said that shit about not looking good in stripes, or what have you, I hit the record button on my phone and placed it in the door panel," Merle said. "It just didn't sit right with me."

Freah nodded. “Me neither.”

“After we left T-Bass’ house, I listened to the recording.” He tapped his thumb on the screen of his phone to play the recording on speaker.

“*Who are you calling*?” came Colleen’s voice.

“*Peggy Sue*,” said Randy.

Freah took a deep breath. Coloring books usually helped her calm her anxiety whenever she either heard about or thought about her parents.

“*Now is not the time for that,*” Colleen said in a tight tone.

“*Would you hush, dammit? If we don’t get this money by tomorrow, we’re gonna lose everything. Now, shush.*”

Freah averted her attention across the street. The sight of Peggy Sue and Jed sickened her. She could never forgive her parents for blatantly ignoring her pleas for help. They did not once punish Franky for molesting her—not even a verbal lashing of disapproval for his outlandish behavior.

“*Hello,*” came Peggy Sue’s voice through the speaker.

“*Hey, Peggy. This Randy. Are you ready to talk?*”

“*Yeah. But maybe it’s best you talk to Jed.*”

“*Alright, well, put ‘em on.*”

Jed’s father passed away and left him a ton of money, and it was at that point that he and Peggy Sue sought sobriety and placed a $100,000 reward out for any information that led to the whereabouts of Franklin Osbourne.

“*This Jed,*” said Freah’s father.

“*You got the money, Jed?*” Randy said.

“*If you think Imma hand over that kinda cash without—*”

Randy interrupted him. “*It’s like I told Peggy yesterday. We know exactly what happened to Franky and where his body is buried.*”

Silence.

Then Jed said, “*And you know this how*?”

“*You’re just gonna have to trust me, boy. A hundred thousand dollars, and no cops.*”

Silence.

"*Don't you and Peggy Sue want justice for Franky?*" Randy said.

"*Of course we—*"

Randy shouted, "*Well, goddammit, act like it, Jed. This ain't no time for games, son.*"

"*I reckon Merle ain't feeding you boys as well as everyone think he is. 'Cause you sound downright desperate, boy.*"

"*You're fishing in the wrong creek, son. How 'bout we just leave Franky where he is? Goodnight.*"

"*No, don't hang up,*" Jed said in a rushed tone. "*Okay. Where you wanna meet?*"

"*How 'bout that Piggly Wiggly right down from—*"

"*I know where it's—*"

"*Right there is fine. I'll text ya' when I'm ready.*"

The call ended.

"*If you screw this money up again, I'm gone, Randy,*" Colleen said. "*I can't keep doing this.*"

"*Woman, don't start with me,*" Randy said in a mocking manner. "*Oh, why my life ain't like Freah's? Why our house ain't big like theirs?*"

"*'Cause it should be, dammit,*" Colleen snapped. "*If you wasn't such a fuck-up, we'd—*"

A smack sounded, and Colleen yelped.

"*You hold your tongue 'bout me, bitch, ya' hear?*"

Silence.

"*Now, this here investment gone make me king 'round here.*"

"*Merle told you it's a bad investment, Randy. Nobody wants a—*"

"*Hush. I know what I know, and this here thang gone work out mighty fine for us, hear?*"

Merle ended the recording, saying to Freah, "Stupid sumbitch don't know his elbow from his asshole."

"He's making her cross us," Freah said in Colleen's defense.

"Reckon if a couple of backhands make yo' cross ya' best friend, your loyalty was never strong enough to stand on its own, nohow."

Freah looked across the street. Colleen was leading the conversation. Merle was right—this was coming off far too easy for Colleen.

"She wants my life," Freah said.

"My pa' always said that a drowning man will clutch at straws."

Freah looked at him. "If we let them do this, we'll lose everything," she said.

Merle nodded. "Including the opportunity to find our son."

Freah's lips tightened as the thought of sitting inside a cold, filthy jail cell while Teddy Lee tortured Errol raced rampantly throughout her mind.

"No," she said quietly. "We can't let that happen."

"No, we can't. So I reckon we gone have ta' place them in the same hole that Franky's in."

Freah looked across the street. "All of 'em," she said firmly.

Merle backed out of the parking space. "I figured you'd understand," he said.

Chapter 26

Errol and Harley loaded the last of the leftover food into the back seat of the truck, then they hurriedly got into the cab themselves. The snow was really coming down and beginning to stick to the roads. Harley turned the heat on and rubbed the palms of her hands together.

"Cold as a witch's titty out here," she said.

Errol chuckled. "I reckon that's pretty damn cold."

"Oh hell yeah. So this food is definitely gone warm some bellies tonight."

Errol pulled out of the lot and headed east, telling Harley, "We need to get some gas."

With a mischievous grin, Harley referred to their sexual energy. "Reckon we burned a whole lotta fuel back yonder." She bit down on her lip seductively.

Errol smiled. "Not enough, if you ask me."

Her eyes flickered with excitement, and she reached for the zipper of his Levi's, but her phone rang—distracting the moment.

With an annoyed sigh, she answered the call. "What do you want, Holly?"

"Where are you?"

Harley made a face. "Uh, none of your—"

"You're with him. Get away from him now, Harley, before you get hurt."

Harley looked at Errol. "What are you talking about, Holly?"

"Just listen, for once, will ya'?"

Holly hung up, and Harley pondered her sister's words, searching for the meaning.

"Everything alright, darling?" Errol asked.

"Yeah. Just . . . Just my sister being weird, is all. I guess, I don't know."

"What gives with you two? Twins are usually inseparable."

Harley sighed. "Holly's stupid. All she cares about is being accepted by folks who will never honestly accept her for who she is."

Harley went on to explain why a wedge was driven between her and Holly, and Errol could hardly believe his ears.

"Impossible," Errol said.

"Nope. She was born that way, is all. But damn, does she hate it. Calls it a curse, and thangs. Likes to take it out on me, like it's my damn fault."

Errol whistled. "That's one hell of a turnip, I tell ya'."

"Reckon she'll come to her senses one day, but right now she's the cork in Derick's ass," she shook her head, disgusted with her sister's antics. "Anything to fit in, I tell ya'."

Errol turned into the gravel lot of a local gas station.

"You want anything from outta here?" he asked her.

"No. Well, some gum, maybe. Yeah."

Errol hopped out the truck and headed for the door. He was floating on cloud nine. Hell, even the snow now had a new meaning to life. Love has a way of making the smaller things seem more fascinating.

Errol has always wanted what his parents had—the step-by-step approach to love, that need for the other's presence, affectionately tolerable with a burning passion to share a valuable existence as one vessel—a family. Now he has that spark with Harley, and every fire begins with a spark.

Minutes later, after filling his tank with gas, Errol got into his truck and kissed Harley deeply on her lips, sensually wet. She took his steam, lapping her tongue over his, swallowing their exchange. His rod stiffened, and her va-jay-jay waved merrily to this arrival of lustful desire.

Her breathing.

His breathing.

Their touch.

Then someone smashed the driver-side window and snatched Errol out the truck.

"Errol!" Harley cried, fumbling with her door handle. "Stop!"

Chapter 27

Rock-on slammed his foot on the brake, and the Mustang fishtailed onto Elton Boulevard with a *skirt, skirt, skirt, scuuuurrrr!* Smoke wafted from the tires as he fought with the steering wheel. Bullets pierced the trunk as the frightening '*Tat, tat, tat, tat*' of an assault rifle rang true. The rear window shattered, causing Rock-on to duck and swerve dangerously. The Mustang sideswiped a parked vehicle—the clamor of wreckage awakened the night.

The wintry wind tossed Rock-on's hair all over his head. He looked in his rearview mirror; they were gaining on him.

More shots fired.

Rock-on cut the wheel and sped onto Benton Avenue with a wide swerve that caused a 360 burnout, slinging the car directly into a tree. The airbag punched him in his face with a jarring effect that rendered him unconscious . . .

As Rock-on came to, he groaned pathetically. His senses were slowly returning. Savannah. Teddy Lee. The high-speed chase. His head throbbed painfully, and he had a massive headache. Voices traveled in and out, as if a mute button was being continuously pressed. And what were these smells? Tobacco? Propane gas? Musk cologne?

Rock-on swallowed the taste of blood. His mouth was dry, and a tooth was missing. Blinking the cobwebs loose, Rock-on absorbed his surroundings, in which he determined that he was in some kind of garage-slash-apartment, maybe.

Someone smacked him across the face, and he nearly toppled over in the chair.

"Wake up," shouted a man. "Potato salad-eating, sumbitch!"

Chapter 28

Doctor Scheffler worked feverishly to save Davie's life, but his patient's vital signs were dropping dramatically, and he had lost a substantial amount of blood. Scheffler slung orders about while carefully trying to extract a bullet from Davie's liver. Nurses did as they were told— injections, oxygen supply, wound detail, and incision assistance—as Scheffler utilized his tools gracefully, hoping to tend to the other two inflictions before it's too late.

An extremely bright light overlooked the surgery, enhancing Davie's damp skin and bluishly white lips. Outside of the occasional twitch of a finger, Davie showed no signs of life.

Davie had always been a fighter, a person who didn't know how to back down, even when, at times, it was best to do so. He had those eyes—eyes like he wasn't afraid of anything—and he wasn't, not until he felt the heat of three bullets tear into his back. While lying face down on that floor, bleeding out, Davie realized for the first time that he hadn't lived, that he had never left southwest Virginia, never married or had children. He had never ridden a plane before, or eaten such foods as sushi, Philly cheesesteak, strawberry lemon biscuits, ratatouille, creole cuisines, and much more. Davie thought of his dream of one day possibly entering a UFC arena and pummeling some poor bastard to death. How had it come to this? An unfulfilled life with nothing to show for it?

Then.

Flatline.

"We're losing him," said a nurse, reaching for the paddles. "Charge!"

Chapter 29

While standing at the border of some pine trees, Freah and Merle quietly watched Jed and Randy shovel into Franky's unmarked grave. The open pasture stretched without any disruptions—not even the common ploy or hay bells throughout the land, just that damn rusty flagpole down by the fence line—a marker in a sense that Colleen obviously remembered.

Freah eyed Colleen evilly, because although she wasn't within earshot of her and her mother's exchange, Freah knew that Colleen was filling in the gaps—relaying the details of that dark, murderous night. Traitors . . . so-called friends, if there ever was a thing, deserved the business end of a pistol. Freah quietly cocked the slide of her Heckler & Koch. When it came to the four people in question, bloodshed meant nothing to her—they would all die tonight.

Freah looked at Merle. He was exhausted. This detrimental situation with Teddy Lee was getting the best of him, because it wasn't about meth or territory with Merle, it was about family and protecting the ones he loved. Errol's current whereabouts were chipping away at him terribly, and now here he was, by her side, helping her clean up her mess again. But that is who Merle is—their savior.

"I love you," Freah said quietly.

Merle looked at her, the moonlight gracing her delicate features perfectly.

"Tell me something I don't know," he said.

They smiled, because he was trying to make light of the moment, and it worked.

"You sure you're okay with this?" he asked her.

Freah wiped a snowflake from her eyelashes, then shifted her gaze to the pasture—Jed and Randy had dug a substantially deep hole—their own grave.

"My folks belonged inside a hole long ago, I reckon," she looked back at him. "Our family is all I want and need, hon."

Merle nodded, then racked the pump on his shotgun, which snagged the ears of their prey. Their confused expressions were answered the moment they spotted two shadowy figures emerge from the grove in a dash. Colleen and Peggy Sue made a run for it.

"Run," shouted Peggy Sue before being gunned down by her very own daughter.

Back at Merle's truck, his phone was ringing. It was Sheriff Dougherty calling about the state of Davie and Squirrel—one just died, and the other was on his way to lockup. Then there was the matter of Rock-on and the suspicious kidnapping by none other than their supposedly dead brother, Dog Man.

Chapter 30

Derick and his two brothers pummeled Errol in a fit of rage, their fists landing with sickening force against his body. Errol tried to shield himself, but his efforts were weak, futile against the brutality of their assault. The pain of their blows, sharp and unrelenting, seared through him, each hit more crushing than the last. His body slammed against the cold, jagged gravel, scraping his skin, while insults rained down on him like a second wave of punishment. The weight of the moment—being torn apart, physically and mentally—brought the harsh reality of revenge to life, as his world blurred with pain and despair.

"She's mine," Derrick growled. "Punk."

Harley grabbed Errol's rifle from the rack and hopped out of the truck. Her heart rate had skyrocketed, but she was far from afraid—she was pissed. Harley ran around the front end of the truck.

"Stop, or I'll fucking shoot," she yelled before popping a round into the air.

The boys all leapt back, frightened, uncertain if one of them had been shot. They looked down at themselves in search of a wound.

An eighteen-wheeler flew past with a heavy gust of wind, projecting the smell of hot brake pads.

Harley leveled the rifle and put them boys in her sights but addressed Errol, saying, "Sweety, you all right?"

Struggling to get to his feet, Errol groaned. "Yeah."

"This ain't right, and you know it, Harley," Derrick said angrily, nostrils as wide as the gates of hell. "You two don't belong—"

"Shut the fuck up, yo' limp dick sumbitch," Harley snapped. "Now, you tree-jumping fucks better get, before I get beside myself and do something I'll regret."

Derrick's features tightened, and he took a step toward her, but his older brother, Curly, placed a hand of caution on his shoulder. Derrick shot him a glare.

"No," was all Curly said.

Errol leaned against his truck while holding his side. His upper lip was busted, and his forehead bore a few knots.

"The endgame is you not being with this—"

Harley cut Derrick off. "Fuck you and your goddamn endgame, you bastard. Take another step and I'll end it right now."

Derrick stared into her eyes. There was no doubt in his mind that Harley would shoot him, and that revelation itself hurt him more than her dating Errol actually had.

Derrick's other brother, Tatum, saw the store clerk peering through the pane glass window at them.

"Let's get outta here before the law come a-knocking," Tatum said.

"I'd listen to 'em, ass wipe," Harley said. "Beat it." She closed an eye and stared down the snout of that big bad rifle. "One," she counted. "Two."

The boys backed away.

"This ain't over, hear?" Derrick threatened.

"You're goddamn right, it's not," Errol responded.

They watched the boys walk across the street to Curly's green pickup, and just when they loaded into the cab, Harley shot the passenger side window out.

"Drive!" they heard one shout.

Curly peeled off and nearly collided into an oncoming vehicle in haste to escape.

"Errrrnnn!" came the blare of the horn.

"A window for a window," Harley shouted.

"You scoundrels get from 'round here!" said the store clerk, who had enough guts to poke his head out the door.

Harley helped Errol to the passenger door. “Get you to the hospital.”

“No,” he said.

“Babe?” she whined.

“No, Harley. It’s nothing but a couple of bumps,” he smiled. “Toughen me up for the NFL, hear?”

She stared at him admiringly. The sign of a strong man turned her on, and she felt her kitty purr.

Harley eased down onto the seat, then handed him the rifle. “You’re gonna get ‘em, ain’t you?” she asked him.

“Does a bear shit in the woods?”

She smiled. “Hell yeah, it does.”

“And correction, lady. We’re gonna get ‘em.”

Harley’s smile reached her eyes. “’Cause from here on out, we’re doing everythang together.”

It was his turn to smile. “I couldn’t have said it better myself, darling.”

They slapped a high five, then Harley ran to get into the truck.

“Where to?” she asked.

“Tent City. Lotta hungry folks to feed.” He used his shirt to blot his lip.

Harley pulled out onto the road and said, “How the hell did they find us?”

She was more so speaking out loud, the thought that crossed her mind.

“Probably was just driving past and seen my truck,” Errol assumed.

Harley considered this. “Yeah, I reckon. Fucking cunt. He’s scared to take you on himself.”

“Most are.”

Harley grinned because she knew this to be true. When she first moved to Norton, all she ever heard about was Errol, and how handsome and athletic he was, but mostly about how he’d fight a room full of rattlesnakes if he had to.

"I saw 'em beat Nathan Childs so bad, the summabitch had to learn his ABC's again," Jack Sauler once told her.

"You think that's something? He whooped Bruce something awful. Mush, you hear me? We could've served Bruce in a punch bowl," Diane Chatum added that day.

Harley looked over at Errol—lip busted, a slight nosebleed, a couple of pump knots, but nothing to cry over, and he wasn't. He was just sitting there as calm as a sunrise. Not easily broken, which was yet another powerful trait that they both shared.

Kitty purred an entire album—she couldn't take it anymore. Pulling over on the side of the road, Harley killed the engine and crawled over the console to her man—settling comfortably on his lap.

Errol smiled. "Howdy, ma'am."

Harley licked her lips. "Hi, sweety."

"Beautiful night, ain't it?"

"Downright gorgeous, hon'."

"All the juke joints in the world—"

She completed his sentence. "I had to walk into yours."

Then she reached down inside his pants and took hold of his stiffness.

Chapter 31

Cunningham smacked Rock-on again, shouting, "Snap to, you yellow-belly sissy. It's foot-to-ass day." He smacked him again.

"Enough," said a familiar voice.

Rock-on looked past Cunningham and saw a ghost. "What the hell?" he murmured, unsure if he was seeing things correctly or not.

"He's taken enough of a beating," Dog Man said.

Cunningham looked at Dog Man with a grit. "Shut the fuck up, before I remind you of that whooping on High Knob Mountain, boy."

Jim Bob, who was leaning against the wall, chuckled. "That's right."

Dog Man shook his head because his body was still healing from the brutal assault he'd undergone that morning in them cold, unforgiving woods . . .

. . . Merle had Dog Man out the front door of his house and onto the porch. The morning air was brisk but freshly invigorating.

While staring out at a couple of cowhands who were rustling a few calves out to pasture, Dog Man took a sip from his coffee mug, then said, "Why do you always have to run shit your way, like we don't have a say in thangs?"

Merle stared down at his coffee mug, the steam carrying the bitter aroma of the coffee beans to his nostrils. He raised the mug to his lips—always the one to think before he spoke, he looked at his brother from over the rim of his cup.

"We're fine right where we are, bub," he finally spoke. "There's no need to branch out any further than we already are."

"See, that's where you're wrong, Merle. There's millions to be made outside this region, and with that recipe of ours, we—"

"Of mine, don't you mean?"

Dog Man's lips tightened, because everyone had always assumed that since he was the one who cooked their meth, it was most likely his recipe, but it was actually Merle's secret concoction of God knows what that he mixed together himself and delivered to Dog Man once a week.

Shaking his head, Dog Man countered Merle's blatant remark. "It's not right that you keep that from us, either. We're your brothers, for Pete's sake. It shows that you don't trust us."

Merle's demeanor didn't differ. "Right. 'Cause my brothers don't benefit at all from my recipe, do they?" he said sarcastically. "Reckon it ain't enough that you boys make more money to choke a mule with, you need more, right?"

"I'm just saying. Towns like Tazewell and Richland are good for the taking, Merle, and we're sitting around here—"

"Doing just fine. Your eyes done got bigger than your stomach, boy. Only a fool sets foot on another man's territory. It's a sure way to put yourself in a pickle, son."

Dog Man waved his hand dismissively. "Bullshit. With the ice we have, we'll be doing them places a favor, by God. They're hot railing straight trash, I tell ya'. I've done my research, boy, and I know what I'm talking about, hear?"

"You're not lis—"

Dog Man cut him off. "You wouldn't even have to show up. I'll make all the trips, Merle. Hell, every mafia from the beginning of time has expanded."

This pissed Merle off, and if Dog Man wasn't his brother, he would've doused his coffee in his face, then commenced knocking his goddamn teeth down his throat.

"We're not a mafia," Merle said tightly. "We're just some good ol' boys with a piece of the pie."

"Wanting the whole pie is what got the mafia wiped off the table."

"Merle, you're not—"

Merle had heard enough, saying, "Take the piece I'm giving you, or take a walk, little brother. I can't let your hare-brained scheme jeopardize everythang we got, boy. I just can't."

Dog Man's nostrils flared. "I've stood by you through thick and thin, Merle. I deserve more respect than what you're handing me, boy."

"I'm not stopping you from branching out. I'm just not going along with you, is all."

"Alright, so give me the mixture, and—"

Merle shook his head. "No. I do this for the family, to put our kids through school and keep the wolf away from the door. No more hungry nights, remember? No more winters without heat, right? And we did that, didn't we? Let's not forget where we came from, boy." He doused his cup of coffee over the banister of the porch. "The only thang you're set on doing is leading the law to my doorstep."

Dog Man watched the door close behind his brother—leaving him boiling hot in the cold. Dog Man hurled his coffee mug out to the driveway and hit Merle's speed boat.

"Son of a bitch," he grumbled, then stormed down the steps of the porch and to his truck.

Speeding out onto the main road, Dog Man hammered the steering wheel with his palm, grunting angrily, pissed at his brother's stubbornness and blatant disregard for what he and the others may want. Dog Man was tired of living in Merle's shadow, taking orders, more so a minion than a partner.

His phone rang. It was his wife, Lisette, calling.

"Hey, hon'," he answered.

"Why ain't you been answering my calls?"

She said,

"Talking with that damn Merle. You know he don't take much of phones, dear."

"Well, some . . . an unholy sort just left here looking for you, and I didn't like the looks of 'em, one bit, I tell you."

Dog Man's heart rate increased, as well as his breathing. He never had visitors at the house, so he knew exactly who they were.

"Say what now?" was all that he could think to say.

"Yeah, some hardnose named Teddy something, and two more bozos come barging in and thangs demanding that I call you," Lisette explained, her tone rushed as if she was on a clock, which she was because she was already late for work. "Said you weren't answering his number or whatnot. What's going on?"

"Did they seem mad to you any?"

"Downright livid. Scared me. Who are they?"

"Couple of honkeys. Nothing to worry about." He managed a lie because there was nothing corny or phony about the 'White Infidels.' They were everything that they were rumored to be—murderous S.C.U.M, which was their acronym for Society Can't Understand Me.

Hearing that Teddy Lee came to his house frightened him. This meant that he was losing his patience and eager to make their next move against Merle—a joint venture that Dog Man was no longer certain about, because there was one person who rattled his cage more than Teddy Lee ever could—Squirrel. If he caught wind of Dog Man's treachery against Merle, Squirrel would surely behead him without a second thought. It would be best if he went at this alone and just kept trying to convince Merle to turn in his direction. He would figure out a way to deal with Teddy Lee and his cronies later. Hopefully.

"Well, I told 'em you probably off somewhere with your brothers," Lisette said, sounding distant as if not speaking directly into her phone.

This caused Dog Man to instinctively look in his mirrors, cursing himself for getting involved with the likes of a biker gang. Some time ago, after overhearing Merle and Randy discussing the near release of Teddy Lee and how he might be an issue for them, Dog Man took it upon himself to visit Teddy Lee at Red Onion prison to get the full length of why his brother feared him so much. It was at this visit that Dog Man decided to team up with Teddy Lee to take over the meth trade in Southwest Virginia—and then beyond.

Dog Man ended the call with Lisette. The conversation with Merle and the news of Teddy Lee's presence in Norton had him at a conflicting interval—at a complete loss. The angel on his shoulder was saying, "Forget all about this and stick by your family." Whereas the demon spoke much louder, more clearly. "To hell with 'em, boy. Take it all for yourself." Then the angel countered, "The Infidels will never allow him to have it all." The demon chuckled. "A couple of planted kilos of meth and an anonymous call to the Feds will put Teddy Lee on a shelf for life."

Dog Man saw a wounded figure up ahead. It appeared to be a man who was walking with a terrible limp.

Dog Man pulled up alongside the man and saw that it was Gene Fleming, one of the many homeless people in Norton who had been affected by the dive of the coal mines.

Rolling the passenger side window down, Dog Man said to Gene, "Say, boy, where ya' headed?"

"To hell if I don't change my ways."

Dog Man smiled. He had always liked Gene and his philosophical sense of self as a drunkard with an imaginary degree in science.

"Reckon I'm going your way, then," Dog Man said. "Hop on in, son."

Gene wasted no time getting in from out of the cold. He stunk to high heaven—a variety of piss, vodka, and mildew.

Dog Man made a face. “Hell fire,” he said, rolling his window down.

“Got a cigarette?” Gene asked him.

Dog Man obliged the man, then pushed forward, bypassing barns and silos on beautifully manicured farmland and rich estates, which prompted Dog Man to question Gene’s presence in such a prestigious area.

“Got a lil’ work up yonder on the Aniston Farm. Folks want me to clear a trench for ‘em. Good pay for an honest day’s work, ya’ know?”

Dog Man agreed. “But it don’t look like you’re in any shape to clear a trench, Gene. That darn leg of yours looks—”

“Worse than what it is. Dang on it, knees like to go out on old Gene from time to time, but I can’t let that stop me. Hell, I need that damn bottle of mine, boy,” he chuckled, referring to vodka. “And folks ‘round here is tight as an ant’s pussy. Not easy to have something just given to you, ya’ know? So . . .” He shrugged and left it at that.

Gene actually came from a good background, with a number of influential family members who were tied into law enforcement and local politics. But despite their unyielding desire to help Gene get back on track, he ignored their voices and did as he pleased—something that actually helped Dog Man put his current dilemma into perspective. He could not allow the so-called notion of family values to overshadow the path of his own.

Dog Man glanced at his side-view mirror and saw a truck closing in on his bumper.

“Shit,” he murmured.

Teddy Lee veered around his truck and sped up alongside them. “Pull over,” he shouted.

Dog Man thought otherwise, but once Cunningham and Jim Bob both extended their pistols outside their windows, he tapped his brake and pulled over onto the dirt.

"Boy, what the sam hell are you doing? Them strangers got guns and thangs. Drive!" Gene exclaimed.

Dog Man stared through the windshield at the approaching men.

"Dog Man, drive, fool. Run them bastards over!" Gene was panicking. "Goddammit, man."

Teddy Lee punched Dog Man in his face, a solid crack that drew blood from his nose.

"Oh," Gene shouted. "Goddamn, man, goddamn."

"Something told me you might be around these parts," Teddy Lee said with a sneer. "Hiding under big brother's skirt." He looked at Cunningham and Jim Bob. "They're coming with us."

. . . "Why?" Rock-on said, snapping Dog Man back to reality. "Why would you do something like this?"

Dog Man brushed past Rock-on's question and asked one of his own. "You and Merle have gotten tighter over the years. If anyone knows, it's you. What's the chemicals he's using to spike the ice?"

"This is wrong, Dog Man, and somewhere inside there you're broken, son."

Dog Man shrugged the analysis off as if it was a mere scarf on his shoulders, saying, "Hell, even a broken clock is right two times a day."

Cunningham punched Rock-on in his mouth, knocking out a tooth.

"Now, Imma ask you again," Dog Man said.

"I'm not Rock-on, dammit. For the last time, already. Y'all got the wrong guy, and he—"

Dog Man punched his brother in his eye, saying, "Sumbitch always been a goddamn liar."

Cunningham and all of the others laughed because they all heard how much of a damn fibber Rock-on was. "Nine times out of ten, if his lips moving, he's fucking lying," was the rumor.

They commenced to beating the crap out of him, but his arguments never deterred.

"I'm not Rock-on!"

Chapter 32

Sheriff Dougherty was seated in his car outside the hospital, polishing his thoughts. Tonight's detail had gotten more complex, more engrossing than any case he had ever worked before, and he was trying to make sense of it all. The people of Inkly Bottom were not prone to cooperation. The dealers controlled that area with fear; even the person who reported the gunshots refused to identify herself. But from the look of that apartment, Dougherty gathered the notion that there were several more people present during the invasion. The place was a sexual cesspool that two people could not have possibly stirred up themselves—not with the various discarded articles of clothing on the floor and the number of erotic toys and lubes they discovered. He had some runners on his hands, and he had to find out who they were.

The electrical doors of the hospital parted, and Dougherty averted his attention to Squirrel, who was being escorted by three of his best deputies to an awaiting cruiser. Squirrel looked at Dougherty with a menacing mug, then hocked a ball of phlegm and spit it on his window.

"Fucking dick-eating vermit," Squirrel shouted. "I'll kill all you sumbitches."

Deputies tightened their hold on him, but were careful not to incite his wound. Squirrel's arm was in a sling—a through-and-through shot that medics easily patched up with a bottle of pain pills to go. Doctors insisted that Squirrel be kept for overnight observation, but Dougherty vehemently opposed their authoritative opinion. Squirrel was a dangerous man who needed to be placed under lock and key.

Dougherty shook his head. He just never seemed to understand the mentality of a criminal—rarely were they smart or sensible. Squirrel was unstable and obviously very capable of cold-blooded murder. A cell is where he belonged . . . for the rest of his natural life.

Dougherty thought back to a magazine article he had read when he was a boy that changed his life and ultimately sealed his decision to become the very first Black Sheriff in Norton. The article was called *Black Law: The History of a Richmond Police Department.* Black officers came together to protect one another against racism in the department in 1988 in Richmond, Virginia, which escalated to violence and eventually to the courts, in which a great number of white cops were prosecuted for hate crimes against members of their fellow badge. It was this publicized chain of events that encouraged Dougherty to want to make a change in Norton and put some color into their department as well as some balance in the scale of justice.

Dougherty looked across the street at the basketball court underneath the tracks. He grew up on this side of town, and he had played ball on that very blacktop a hundred times. Although things were rough back then, it wasn't nearly as bad as it is now. The dealers who loitered on the bleachers in and around the fence indicated as much. The town had gone from sugar to shit. Was he really making a difference as Sheriff? Maybe the assassination of Merle and his brothers would lessen the flow of ice in the area—maybe.

Dougherty's phone rang. It was Patrick calling.

"What you got for me, son?" Dougherty answered, referring to the body that they uprooted from Dog Man's grave.

"The DNA analysis came . . ." Patrick's words trailed, kind of choked a bit.

"Patrick?" Dougherty was concerned.

"I'm here," he cleared his throat uncomfortably. "Dad, it's Gene."

"What?"

"Yeah."

Patrick relayed the details of their findings. Tears raced down Dougherty's face. This changed everything. Within a minute of that phone call, Dougherty went from wanting to put folks in jail to wanting to put folks into the ground. Not poor Gene. Gene had never once harmed a hair on any gent's head or spoke sideways to an approaching lady on an evening strut. He was always helpful and polite. Gene resided in Tent City, a large community of tight-knit people who would surely know the details of the last 24 hours of Gene's existence, because he was not a user and had no business whatsoever with Dog Man.

"And from what we gathered from the Burger Shack, I reckon it's safe to assume that Dog Man killed Gene in pursuit of staging his own death," Patrick said.

"Yeah. But why Gene, of all people? They don't even move in the same circle."

"Could be personal, pop."

Dougherty sniffed. "Real damn personal. Reckon we should've seen this a while ago."

"Bastard," Patrick said quietly.

Dougherty got out of the car. He needed some fresh air. He walked to the far end of the building. The jitters had a hold of him. He was boiling with rage, stewing in pain—murderously set on vengeance. Gene's death would not be in vain. Not if he had anything to do with it.

"Pa'?"

Dougherty took a deep breath. "I'm here, son," then wiped his eyes.

"We need to find Dog Man."

Dougherty headed back toward the front. "Reckon Merle would be the next mark."

"Hmm. Think he got the balls to try the big man?"

"He already has."

"Right." Patrick agreed.

"Why? I don't know why, but by George, the sumbitch ain't gonna win. Merle's the slipperiest rascal this side of Virginia, I tell ya', and as soon as he catches wind of this here shit, you best believe he's gonna set a snare trap that's gonna break at the knees."

"And we're gonna be there when it happens."

"Darn tootin', we are."

At that instant, Merle's pickup truck sped into the lot recklessly and bustled toward the entrance. Dougherty left a voicemail on Merle's phone about his brothers and the shooting in Inkly Bottom. Davie died twice on the operating table but was miraculously looking to survive his gunshot injuries. This family was ducking the presence of death by mere inches.

"Speaking of the devil," Dougherty said to Patrick. "Merle just pulled in."

Merle and Freah hopped out of the truck and ran for the doors of the emergency room. Dougherty immediately noticed how dirty they both were. It wasn't uncommon to see farmyard owners caked in dirt, but Freah and Merle employed a substantial amount of help on their property and never indulged in manual labor personally, so their current appearance was beyond suspicious.

"Hold on, son," Dougherty said, lowering the phone from his ear.

Merle and Freah dashed through the doors without even a mere glance in Dougherty's direction. Dougherty walked to the truck to inspect the cab and bed and immediately saw a phone lying on the console and a pistol nested in the nook of the passenger seat.

Red flags, if he ever saw any. Dougherty opened the driver's side door to retrieve both items. Merle and Freah would assume that the hoods across the street stole their belongings—naturally.

Dougherty placed his phone to his ear. "I need you to get to the hospital, son," he said. "There will be a gun and a phone in my glove box. Get ‘em and take ‘em back to the station.”

“Uh, okay. What’s going on?” Patrick wanted to know.

“I got ‘em from Merle’s truck. Something ain’t right here, but I’ll fill you in later. Right now, I wanna know everywhere this damn phone has been in the last two hours, because from the looks of things, they might’ve already killed Dog Man.”

“Okay. And what are you gonna do?”

“What every decent lawman does. Console the victim’s family and reassure that justice shall prevail.”

Dougherty ended the call, then grumbled. “Fucking white boys.”

To Be Continued…

Lock Down Publications and Ca$h Presents Assisted Publishing Packages

Due to an increase in the price of services we have increased our prices. The prices below reflect the price increase as of 11/1/24.

BASIC PACKAGE **$699** Editing Cover Design Formatting	**UPGRADED PACKAGE** **$1000** Typing Editing Cover Design Formatting Upload eBooks to Amazon Upload Paperback to Amazon

ADVANCE PACKAGE	LDP SUPREME PACKAGE
$1,400	**$1,700**
Typing	Typing
Editing (line editing/content)	Editing (line editing/content)
Cover Design	Cover Design
Formatting	Formatting
Copyright Registration	Copyright Registration
Proofreading	Proofreading
Upload eBooks to Amazon	Set up Amazon Account
Upload Paperback to Amazon	Upload eBooks to Amazon
	Upload Paperback to Amazon
	Advertise on LDP's Amazon and Facebook Page

***

Other services available upon request.
Additional charges may apply

Lock Down Publications
P.O. Box 944
Stockbridge, GA 30281-9998
Phone: 470 303-9761
Email: lockdownpublications@gmail.com

Submission Guideline

Submit the first three chapters of your completed manuscript to ldpsubmissions@gmail.com. In the subject line add **Your Book's Title**. The manuscript must be in a Word Doc file and sent as an attachment. Document should be in Times New Roman, double spaced, and in size 12 font. Also, provide your synopsis and full contact information. If sending multiple submissions, they must each be in a separate email.

Have a story but no way to send it electronically? You can still submit to LDP/Ca$h Presents. Send in the first three chapters, written or typed, of your completed manuscript to:

LDP: Submissions Dept
P.O. Box 944
Stockbridge, GA 30281-9998

DO NOT send original manuscript. Must be a duplicate. Provide your synopsis and a cover letter containing your full contact information.

Thanks for considering LDP and Ca$h Presents.

NEW RELEASES

BLOODLINE OF A SAVAGE 1-3
THESE VICIOUS STREETS 1-3
RELENTLESS GOON 1-3
BY PRINCE A. TAUHID

THE BUTTERFLY MAFIA 1-3
BY FUMIYA PAYNE

A THUG'S STREET PRINCESS 1&2
BY MEESHA

CITY OF SMOKE 3
BY MOLOTTI

GET IT IN SLUGS 1 &2
BY B. STALL

STANDING ON HER BUSINESS 1&2
BY DG SANTANA

STEPPERS 1,2&3
THE REAL BADDIES OF CHI-RAQ
BY KING RIO

THE LANE 1&2
BY KEN-KEN SPENCE

THUG OF SPADES 1&2
LOVE IN THE TRENCHES 2
CORNER BOYS
BY COREY ROBINSON

TIL DEATH 3
BY ARYANNA

THE BIRTH OF A GANGSTER 4
BY DELMONT PLAYER

PRODUCT OF THE STREETS 1-3
BY DEMOND "MONEY" ANDERSON

NO TIME FOR ERROR
BY KEESE

MONEY HUNGRY DEMONS 1-2
BY TRANAY ADAMS

HUB CITY MENACE 1-3

WHITE BOYS | BANDEMIC

BY J. WHITE

A THUGGISH PASSION 1&2
LAND OF DA HOOLIGANZ 1-4
KILLAZ ON STANDBY 1&2
BY IRA B.

FO'EVA ROLLIN 1&2
BY ASSA RAYMOND BAKER

THE LEVEL UP 1&3
BY LUXURY KING

Coming Soon from Lock Down Publications/Ca$h Presents

IF YOU CROSS ME ONCE 6
ANGEL V
By Anthony Fields

A THUGS STREET PRINCESS 3
By Meesha

CORNER BOYS 2

WHITE BOYS | BANDEMIC

By Corey Robinson

THA TAKEOVER
By Keith Chandler

BETRAYAL OF A G 2
By Ray Vinci

SAVAGE FAMILY EMPIRE 1&2
SOULLESS GOON 1,2&3
THE DIRTY SIDE OF MONEY 1,2&3
By Prince

FOR MY ENEMY'S SAKE
AMBITIONS OF A SLIDER
FRESH OFF DA PORCH
By IRA B.

BY THE TRUCKLOAD 1-4
TIPPIN' THE SCALES 1-3
BAD BITCHES WIT GUNZ 3
PROBLEM SOLVED 2
By Christopher "Diesel" Hornezes

Available Now

RESTRAINING ORDER 1 & 2
By **CA$H & Coffee**

LOVE KNOWS NO BOUNDARIES 1-3
By **Coffee**

RAISED AS A GOON I, II, III & IV
BRED BY THE SLUMS I, II, III
BLAST FOR ME I & II
ROTTEN TO THE CORE I II III
A BRONX TALE I, II, III

WHITE BOYS | BANDEMIC

DUFFLE BAG CARTEL I II III IV V VI
HEARTLESS GOON I II III IV V
A SAVAGE DOPEBOY I II
DRUG LORDS I II III
CUTTHROAT MAFIA I II
KING OF THE TRENCHES
By **Ghost**

LAY IT DOWN I & II
LAST OF A DYING BREED I II
BLOOD STAINS OF A SHOTTA I & II III
By **Jamaica**

LOYAL TO THE GAME I II III
LIFE OF SIN I, II III
By **TJ & Jelissa**

IF LOVING HIM IS WRONG…I & II
LOVE ME EVEN WHEN IT HURTS I II III
By **Jelissa**

PUSH IT TO THE LIMIT
By **Bre' Hayes**

BLOODY COMMAS I & II
SKI MASK CARTEL I, II & III
KING OF NEW YORK I II, III IV V
RISE TO POWER I II III
COKE KINGS I II III IV V
BORN HEARTLESS I II III IV
KING OF THE TRAP I II
By **T.J. Edwards**

WHEN THE STREETS CLAP BACK I & II III
THE HEART OF A SAVAGE I II III IV
MONEY MAFIA I II
LOYAL TO THE SOIL I II III
By **Jibril Williams**

A DISTINGUISHED THUG STOLE MY HEART I II & III
LOVE SHOULDN'T HURT I II III IV
RENEGADE BOYS 1-4
PAID IN KARMA 1-3
SAVAGE STORMS 1-3
AN UNFORESEEN LOVE 1-3
BABY, I'M WINTERTIME COLD 1-3
A THUG'S STREET PRINCESS 1&2
By **Meesha**

A GANGSTER'S CODE 1-3
A GANGSTER'S SYN 1-3
THE SAVAGE LIFE 1-3
CHAINED TO THE STREETS 1-3
BLOOD ON THE MONEY 1-3
A GANGSTA'S PAIN 1-3
BEAUTIFUL LIES AND UGLY TRUTHS
CHURCH IN THESE STREETS
By **J-Blunt**

CUM FOR ME 1-8
An LDP Erotica Collaboration

BLOOD OF A BOSS 1-5
SHADOWS OF THE GAME
TRAP BASTARD
By **Askari**

THE STREETS BLEED MURDER 1-3
THE HEART OF A GANGSTA 1-3
By **Jerry Jackson**

WHEN A GOOD GIRL GOES BAD
By **Adrienne**

THE COST OF LOYALTY 1-3
By **Kweli**

BRIDE OF A HUSTLA 1-3
THE FETTI GIRLS 1-3
CORRUPTED BY A GANGSTA 1-4
BLINDED BY HIS LOVE
THE PRICE YOU PAY FOR LOVE 1-3
DOPE GIRL MAGIC 1-3
By **Destiny Skai**

A KINGPIN'S AMBITION
A KINGPIN'S AMBITION II
I MURDER FOR THE DOUGH
By **Ambitious**

TRUE SAVAGE 1-7
DOPE BOY MAGIC 1-3
MIDNIGHT CARTEL 1-3
CITY OF KINGZ 1&2
NIGHTMARE ON SILENT AVE
THE PLUG OF LIL MEXICO 1&2
CLASSIC CITY
By **Chris Green**

A GANGSTER'S REVENGE 1-4
THE BOSS MAN'S DAUGHTERS 1-5
A SAVAGE LOVE 1&2
BAE BELONGS TO ME 1&2
A HUSTLER'S DECEIT 1-3
WHAT BAD BITCHES DO 1-3
SOUL OF A MONSTER 1-3
KILL ZONE
A DOPE BOY'S QUEEN 1-3
TIL DEATH 1-3
IMMA DIE BOUT MINE 1-6
DYING FOR LIKES
By **Aryanna**

WHITE BOYS | BANDEMIC

A DOPEBOY'S PRAYER
By **Eddie "Wolf" Lee**

THE KING CARTEL 1-3
By **Frank Gresham**

THESE NIGGAS AIN'T LOYAL 1-3
By **Nikki Tee**

GANGSTA SHYT 1-3
By **CATO**

THE ULTIMATE BETRAYAL
By **Phoenix**

BOSS'N UP 1-3
By **Royal Nicole**

I LOVE YOU TO DEATH
By **Destiny J**

I RIDE FOR MY HITTA
I STILL RIDE FOR MY HITTA
By **Misty Holt**

LOVE & CHASIN' PAPER
By **Qay Crockett**

TO DIE IN VAIN
SINS OF A HUSTLA
By **ASAD**

BROOKLYN HUSTLAZ
By **Boogsy Morina**

BROOKLYN ON LOCK 1 & 2
By **Sonovia**

GANGSTA CITY

WHITE BOYS | BANDEMIC

By **Teddy Duke**

A DRUG KING AND HIS DIAMOND 1-3
A DOPEMAN'S RICHES
HER MAN, MINE'S TOO 1&2
CASH MONEY HO'S
THE WIFEY I USED TO BE 1&2
PRETTY GIRLS DO NASTY THINGS
By **Nicole Goosby**

LIPSTICK KILLAH 1-3
CRIME OF PASSION 1-3
FRIEND OR FOE 1-3
By **Mimi**

TRAPHOUSE KING 1-3
KINGPIN KILLAZ 1-3
STREET KINGS 1&2
PAID IN BLOOD 1&2
CARTEL KILLAZ 1-3
DOPE GODS 1&2
By **Hood Rich**

THE STREETS ARE CALLING
By **Duquie Wilson**

STEADY MOBBN' 1-3
THE STREETS STAINED MY SOUL 1-3
By **Marcellus Allen**

WHO SHOT YA 1-3
SON OF A DOPE FIEND 1-4
HEAVEN GOT A GHETTO 1&2
SKI MASK MONEY 1&2
By **Renta**

GORILLAZ IN THE BAY 1-4
TEARS OF A GANGSTA 1/&2
3X KRAZY 1&2

WHITE BOYS | BANDEMIC

STRAIGHT BEAST MODE 1&2
By **DE'KARI**

TRIGGADALE 1-3
MURDA WAS THE CASE 1-3
By **Elijah R. Freeman**

SLAUGHTER GANG 1-3
RUTHLESS HEART 1-3
By **Willie Slaughter**

GOD BLESS THE TRAPPERS 1-3
THESE SCANDALOUS STREETS 1-3
FEAR MY GANGSTA 1-5
THESE STREETS DON'T LOVE NOBODY 1-2
BURY ME A G 1-5
A GANGSTA'S EMPIRE 1-4
THE DOPEMAN'S BODYGAURD 1&2
THE REALEST KILLAZ 1-3
THE LAST OF THE OGS 1-3
By **Tranay Adams**

MARRIED TO A BOSS 1-3
By **Destiny Skai & Chris Green**

KINGZ OF THE GAME 1-7
CRIME BOSS 1-4
By **Playa Ray**

FUK SHYT
By **Blakk Diamond**

DON'T F#CK WITH MY HEART 1&2
By **Linnea**

ADDICTED TO THE DRAMA 1-3
IN THE ARM OF HIS BOSS
By **Jamila**

LOYALTY AIN'T PROMISED 1&2
By **Keith Williams**

YAYO 1-4
A SHOOTER'S AMBITION 1&2
BRED IN THE GAME
By **S. Allen**

TRAP GOD 1-3
RICH $AVAGE 1-3
MONEY IN THE GRAVE 1-3
CARTEL MONEY 1&2
By **Martell Troublesome Bolden**

FOREVER GANGSTA 1&2
GLOCKS ON SATIN SHEETS 1&2
By **Adrian Dulan**

TOE TAGZ 1-4
LEVELS TO THIS SHYT 1&2
IT'S JUST ME AND YOU
By **Ah'Million**

KINGPIN DREAMS 1-3
RAN OFF ON DA PLUG
By **Paper Boi Rari**

THE STREETS MADE ME 1-3
By **Larry D. Wright**

CONFESSIONS OF A GANGSTA 1-4
CONFESSIONS OF A JACKBOY 1-3
CONFESSIONS OF A HITMAN
CONFESSIONS OF A DOPE BOY
By **Nicholas Lock**

I'M NOTHING WITHOUT HIS LOVE

WHITE BOYS | BANDEMIC

SINS OF A THUG
TO THE THUG I LOVED BEFORE
A GANGSTA SAVED XMAS
IN A HUSTLER I TRUST
By **Monet Dragun**

QUIET MONEY 1-3
THUG LIFE 1-3
EXTENDED CLIP 1&2
A GANGSTA'S PARADISE
By **Trai'Quan**

CAUGHT UP IN THE LIFE 1-3
THE STREETS NEVER LET GO 1-3
By **Robert Baptiste**

NEW TO THE GAME 1-3
MONEY, MURDER & MEMORIES 1-3
By **Malik D. Rice**

CREAM 2-3
THE STREETS WILL TALK
By **Yolanda Moore**

THE STREETS WILL NEVER CLOSE 1-3
By **K'ajji**

LIFE OF A SAVAGE 1-4
A GANGSTA'S QUR'AN 1-4
MURDA SEASON 1-3
GANGLAND CARTEL 1-3
CHI'RAQ GANGSTAS 1-4
KILLERS ON ELM STREET 1-3
JACK BOYZ N DA BRONX 1-3
A DOPEBOY'S DREAM 1-3
JACK BOYS VS DOPE BOYS 1-3
COKE GIRLZ
COKE BOYS

WHITE BOYS | BANDEMIC

SOSA GANG 1&2
BRONX SAVAGES
BODYMORE KINGPINS
BLOOD OF A GOON
By **Romell Tukes**

CONCRETE KILLA 1-3
VICIOUS LOYALTY 1-3
BLOODY MONEY BAGS
By **Kingpen**

THE ULTIMATE SACRIFICE 1-6
KHADIFI
IF YOU CROSS ME ONCE 1-3
ANGEL 1-4
IN THE BLINK OF AN EYE
By **Anthony Fields**

THE LIFE OF A HOOD STAR
By **Ca$h & Rashia Wilson**

NIGHTMARES OF A HUSTLA 1-3
BLOOD AND GAMES 1&2
By **King Dream**

GHOST MOB
By **Stilloan Robinson**

HARD AND RUTHLESS 1&2
MOB TOWN 251
THE BILLIONAIRE BENTLEYS 1-3
REAL G'S MOVE IN SILENCE
By **Von Diesel**

MOB TIES 1-7
SOUL OF A HUSTLER, HEART OF A KILLER 1-3
GORILLAZ IN THE TRENCHES
OOPS CRY TOO 1&2
THE DAUGHTER OF A CARTEL BOSS

WHITE BOYS | BANDEMIC

By **SayNoMore**

BODYMORE MURDERLAND 1-3
THE BIRTH OF A GANGSTER 1-4
By **Delmont Player**

FOR THE LOVE OF A BOSS 1&2
By **C. D. Blue**

KILLA KOUNTY 1-5
TENDER
By **Khufu**

MOBBED UP 1-4
THE BRICK MAN 1-5
THE COCAINE PRINCESS 1-10
STEPPERS 1-3
SUPER GREMLIN 1-4
A GANGSTA'S SON
By **King Rio**

MONEY GAME 1&2
By **Smoove Dolla**

A GANGSTA'S KARMA 1-5
By **FLAME**

KING OF THE TRENCHES 1-3
By **GHOST & TRANAY ADAMS**

BAD BITCHES WIT GUNZ 1&2
PROBLEM SOLVED
By "Christopher Diesel" Hornezes

QUEEN OF THE ZOO 1&2
By **Black Migo**

GRIMEY WAYS 1-3

WHITE BOYS | BANDEMIC

BETRAYAL OF A G
By **Ray Vinci**

XMAS WITH AN ATL SHOOTER
By **Ca$h & Destiny Skai**

KING KILLA 1&2
By **Vincent "Vitto" Holloway**

BETRAYAL OF A THUG 1&2
By **Fre$h**

COUNTDOWN OF A KILLA 1&2
SEX, MURDER AND GOD 1&2
GUNS DOWN, BOTTOMS UP 1&2
By Lo-Life

THE MURDER QUEENS 1-7
By **Michael Gallon**

FOR THE LOVE OF BLOOD 1-4
By **Jamel Mitchell**

HOOD CONSIGLIERE 1&2
NO TIME FOR ERROR
By **Keese**

PROTÉGÉ OF A LEGEND 1,2&3
LOVE IN THE TRENCHES 1&2
By **Corey Robinson**

THE PLUG'S RUTHLESS DAUGHTER 1&2
By **Tony Daniels**

BORN IN THE GRAVE 1-3
CRIME PAYS
By **Self Made Tay**

MOAN IN MY MOUTH
By **XTASY**

TORN BETWEEN A GANGSTER AND A GENTLEMAN
By **J-BLUNT & Miss Kim**

LOYALTY IS EVERYTHING 1-3
CITY OF SMOKE 1-3
By **Molotti**

HERE TODAY GONE TOMORROW 1&2
By **Fly Rock**

WOMEN LIE MEN LIE 1-4
FIFTY SHADES OF SNOW 1-3
STACK BEFORE YOU SPLURGE
GIRLS FALL LIKE DOMINOES
NAÏVE TO THE STREETS
By **ROY MILLIGAN**

PILLOW PRINCESS
By **S. Hawkins**

THE BUTTERFLY MAFIA 1-3
SALUTE MY SAVAGERY 1&2
By **Fumiya Payne**

THE LANE 1&2
By Ken-Ken Spence

THE PUSSY TRAP 1-5
By **Nene Capri**

DIRTY DNA
By **Blaque**

SANCTIFIED AND HORNY

WHITE BOYS | BANDEMIC

by **XTASY**

BOOKS BY LDP'S CEO, CA$H

TRUST IN NO MAN
TRUST IN NO MAN 2
TRUST IN NO MAN 3
BONDED BY BLOOD
SHORTY GOT A THUG
THUGS CRY
THUGS CRY 2
THUGS CRY 3
TRUST NO BITCH
TRUST NO BITCH 2
TRUST NO BITCH 3
TIL MY CASKET DROPS

WHITE BOYS | BANDEMIC

RESTRAINING ORDER
RESTRAINING ORDER 2
IN LOVE WITH A CONVICT
LIFE OF A HOOD STAR
XMAS WITH AN ATL SHOOTER

www.ingramcontent.com/pod-product-compliance
Lightning Source LLC
LaVergne TN
LVHW010915110826
845149LV00013B/2364

9781971770079